The Pet-Sitting Peril

Willo Davis Roberts

THE
PET-SITTING
PERIL

Atheneum New York

Library of Congress Cataloging in Publication Data

Roberts, Willo Davis.
    The Pet-sitting Peril.

    Summary: A boy who pet-sits in an apartment house
becomes suspicious when too many fires happen in
the building.
    [1. Arson—Fiction. 2. Crime and criminals—Fiction.
3. Apartment houses—Fiction] I. Title.
PZ7.R54465Pe   1983   [Fic]   82-13757
ISBN 0-689-30963-5

Atheneum
Macmillan Publishing Company
866 Third Avenue, New York, NY 10022
Collier Macmillan Canada, Inc.

Composition by American-Stratford Graphic Services, Inc.
Brattleboro, Vermont
Manufactured by Fairfield Graphics,
Fairfield, Pennsylvania

First Edition

5 7 9 11 13 15 17 19 F/C 20 18 16 14 12 10 8 6

To MY GRANDCHILDREN, *readers all*

The Pet-Sitting Peril

I

THE hall light was out again.

Nick saw that as soon as he rounded the corner. He broke stride, though the dog continued to pull him along in spite of himself. It was the third time in a week, he thought uneasily. This was Thursday, and it had been out on Monday, and last week Friday. Why did that light keep going out?

It wasn't that he was afraid of the dark, like a little kid. After all, he was nearly twelve. It was only that it seemed peculiar for a light bulb not to last more than a few days at a time; and that entry hall was sure black when the light wasn't on.

There was still a glow in Mr. Haggard's first floor apartment to the right of the double doors. The middle part of the big window was ordinary glass, but it was surrounded by a border of multicolored glass segments that glowed like jewels when the light came through them. There was colored glass like that around the windows in the doors, too; and when the hall light was

3

on you could read the big numbers of the house on the glass: twelve on one side, thirty on the other.

Twelve-thirty Hillsdale Street. In the daytime you could read the sign secured to one of the posts that held up the porch roof: Hillsdale Apartments. Now you couldn't tell there was a sign on the porch, let alone read it, because the outside porch light was out, too.

It was almost as if someone were deliberately unscrewing the bulbs, Nick thought, stepping off the opposite curb as Rudy tugged on the leash. Only why would anyone do that? And how? Since the outside doors were locked, nobody could enter except the residents who had keys.

He wondered if Dad would let him bring a flashlight with him at night from now on, the little one that would fit in his pocket. He'd ask tomorrow.

Rudy, not in the least tired although they'd been gone for over an hour, strained to cross the street and bound up the steps onto the dark porch. Rudy was an Airedale, and he weighed eighty-five pounds, so when he pulled against Nick's small frame there wasn't much choice except to move with him.

Nick had the key ready in his hand, sorted out while he was under the streetlight. He unlocked the door and heard a short "whuff" from Rudy that might have been a warning. Nick stood still, his heart pounding unaccountably; Rudy didn't bark again, and after a few seconds there was the sound of a door closing, somewhere far back in the building.

"Is somebody here?" Nick asked, and felt silly when no one answered. Rudy was again tugging him along, toward Mr. Haggard's apartment; he could find that without any lights—it was only a matter of putting out

4

his free hand until he felt the doorknob. Of course nobody was in the hallway with him, or Rudy would know it. Dogs could tell that kind of thing.

Still, there had been that odd half-bark when Nick first opened the front door. Rudy had never done that before, and Nick had been walking him for almost three weeks now, twice a day, every day. There must have been some reason for it.

He had a little trouble getting the key into Mr. Haggard's door, because he couldn't see the lock and Rudy was too eager to get inside and receive his treat. He always got a bone-shaped dog biscuit when they returned from a walk.

"Sit," Nick commanded, and was relieved when the dog obeyed so that he could finally insert the key and twist it.

It seemed bright in the big, cluttered room when they first walked into it. Mr. Haggard was seated in his chair with a blanket over his legs, reading the evening paper.

"Have a nice walk?" he asked, pushing his glasses into place on his nose.

"More of a run, it was," Nick said, slipping the choke chain over Rudy's head so he could go for his "cookie," as Mr. Haggard referred to the treats. "We ran all the way around the park. The light's out in the hall."

"Again?" The old man shook his head. "They don't make anything that lasts any more. We'll have to tell Mr. Griesner to replace it again. You in a hurry, boy? You care to make us each a cup of cocoa before you go? And there's a package of cookies on the counter, there."

Nick liked Mr. Haggard. He seemed to be about eighty years old, and he was sort of shriveled up so that his clothes all seemed a little bit too big on him. He had wispy white hair around a pink bald spot, and there were blue veins showing in his hands. When his leg was hurting, his voice wasn't very strong. But he had a nice smile and he was kind. Anybody could see that he loved Rudy.

"Only family I got left," Mr. Haggard had said, dropping a hand to caress the big shaggy head. "Almost ten years old. That's seventy years in man years, you know. Rudy's getting old, the same as me."

"He doesn't seem old," Nick said, and it was true. "He's strong enough to pull me along whether I want to go or not, especially if he takes me off guard."

Mr. Haggard chuckled. "He'll usually mind if you tell him to *sit*. He's been through obedience school, Rudy has. Airedales are hard to train, though, and they don't always do what you want. Not, you understand, that Airedales aren't smart. They're plenty smart. The thing is, you have to make them want to do the same thing as *you* want. They have to see the advantage to themselves before they do it. That's one reason I give Rudy a cookie when he comes back from a walk. To reward him for taking me along, you see?"

Nick wasn't sure he saw, but what the heck, this was a job, and he hadn't turned up anything before this. Everybody had looked at him, ignored his age, and decided he was too small for whatever they wanted done, even when the jobs didn't require any special strength. Not as much muscle as this job took, actually.

He brought the cocoa, topped by two fat marshmallows in each cup, and the package of cookies. Store bought ones, but fairly good, nevertheless. "Rudy acted funny when we came in," he said. He'd been debating whether or not to mention it all the time he fixed the

6

cocoa. "He sort of 'whuffed' when I opened the front door, as if there was someone inside. And then I heard a door close way in the back of the house. Rudy didn't bark any more, so I didn't know if there was somebody inside that didn't belong here or not. We made enough noise coming up the steps so they had plenty of warning, if anybody didn't want us to see them."

Mr. Haggard looked at him thoughtfully, warming his hand on the cup of cocoa. "Why would anybody want to hide from you? Couldn't be anybody inside unless they had a key. The door was locked the way it's supposed to be, wasn't it?"

"Yes. Only Rudy's never made that kind of noise before. I thought he was reacting to something."

Mr. Haggard sipped melted marshmallow off the top of his drink. "More'n likely he was reacting to one of those confounded cats. I doubt he'd actually hurt one of 'em, but he always dives for a cat when he sees one. You have to brace your feet to hold him."

"I know. He pulled me into a stack of garbage cans in the alley, chasing a cat. Yeah, maybe that was it. One of the cats was there in the hallway."

Later, though, walking home through the chilly night air that was typical of the Northern California coastal area where he lived, Nick wondered. If it was a cat, then who had closed the door, far back there in the dark?

In the daytime, Hillsdale was an ordinary looking street, though quite different from the one Nick lived on only four blocks away. The Chamber of Commerce handed out brochures to tourists, telling of the interesting things to be seen in town and around it: the beaches; the museum; the fish hatchery; the magnificent house built many years ago by a millionaire in the lumber and shipping business, and Hillsdale Street, two blocks long and lined with Victorian houses, most of them nearly a hundred years old. Once they had been grand, elegant family mansions. Now most had been converted to apartments and rooming houses. The one at 1230 had been divided into five apartments, including the one at the first floor back where Mr. Griesner lived. Mr. Griesner enjoyed a reduction in his rent in exchange for maintaining the place and collecting the rents for the owner; he was supposed to see to things like light bulbs in the hallways.

Nick had talked to Mr. Griesner once, the first time the lower hall light went out. The man came to the door in dirty greasy pants and a soiled undershirt, tall and skinny with a head of fuzzy gray hair and a sour expression. He wasn't very happy about having his TV viewing interrupted, but he'd fixed the light. Only it didn't seem to stay fixed very long.

A couple of Sundays ago, on their way home from church, the Reeds had driven down Hillsdale so Nick's family could see where it was he'd taken the job of caring for Rudy.

"I love these old houses," Mrs. Reed said. "Imagine, having seven bedrooms and four bathrooms! We'd never have to line up again!"

"Imagine," Mr. Reed said less enthusiastically, "having to pay the heating bills on one of those places. They had fourteen-foot ceilings downstairs, ten-foot ceilings upstairs, Louise. Even in this climate, it would take my whole salary to keep the place warm."

"I know. It's only a daydream, to have all that space. Aren't they lovely old houses, though?"

Most of them were similar in style to the Hillsdale Apartments. Very tall, narrow buildings, two stories high with an attic above that made another full floor if anybody wanted to finish it. Some, like 1230, had widow's walks atop them. This was a flat area surrounded by a wrought-iron fence where, Mr. Reed said, the women had paced as they watched for their men to return from the sea. "From up there, they could see the mouth of the harbor, and they recognized all the local ships, which were gone for weeks or even months at a time."

"I wouldn't have liked that part of it," Nick's mother admitted, craning to see the upper part of the house they were passing. "Look at the gingerbread on that one! All those fancy shapes cut in the wood, curlicues and birds and geometric designs. You know, I think the one where you work, Nick, would be among the prettiest ones, if it had a fresh coat of paint."

The houses were certainly different from the ones on Groves Street, where the Reeds had lived ever since Nick was four years old. The houses there were modern and convenient, if not so spacious.

His family reassured about the area where he was going every day, no one said any more about it not being safe for Nick to be there after dark. It was, except for the age and size of the houses, an ordinary neighborhood like his own.

"Do you know how long this job will last?" Nick's father had asked as they turned into their own street.

"As long as Mr. Haggard can't walk very well, I guess. His leg hurts quite a bit, I think; when I'm there, he has me get things for him instead of walking across the room for them. Rudy needs a lot of exercise, and he helps me practice my running, so it's working out all right."

Winnie piped up from the back seat of the station wagon. "Do you think we're going to have enough money to go to Disneyland before school starts, Daddy?"

Winnie was seven, the youngest in the family, and Nick's favorite. She never made fun of him or tried to provoke him into a fight, the way Barney did, and she didn't ignore him, the way Charles and Molly often did. Winnie thought he was clever and brave and strong. She had been talking about Disneyland for a long time.

Usually the whole family went together on great camping trips, either to the beach or to the Trinity Alps, and once they'd gone to Yosemite, though there had been too many people there to satisfy the Reeds' yearning for wilderness. This year, though, Dad said he had to paint the house and put a new roof on it, or they'd never make it through another rainy winter. And the cost of gas had risen so high that going anywhere very far from home was too expensive to think about. Dad was a teacher, and teachers didn't make all that much. Even with his mother working, funds were tight.

Disneyland was a long way off. People in other places thought if you lived in California you must be right next door to Disneyland, but from where the Reeds lived it was over 800 miles. Before Mr. Reed could get his mouth open to point that out, Winnie said with a smile, "Everybody has a job now, except me, and I'll give my allowance. If everybody saved their money to pay for the gas, couldn't we go, Daddy?"

They'd looked at each other, torn between the lure of a vacation and the sacrifice it would take.

Molly was the first to speak. Molly was the oldest, at

seventeen, and she had a full time job all summer, taking care of two little boys while their mother worked. "I need a new coat for school, and I'd have to keep a little out for movies and skating. But . . ." She hesitated, then made an offer that astounded her brothers. "I'll put seventy-five per cent of what I make into a Disneyland fund, if the boys will do it, too."

Charles, who worked at a hamburger place, did some quick calculations. "Well, I guess I could do that, too. How about you, Barney? You lined up enough lawns to mow to do us any good?"

Nick had seen the chart Barney had made, with a column for each day of the week, divided into hours, with names written in for each place he was to cut the grass. Barney was fourteen and considerably taller and heavier than Nick; he was saving for a motorcycle when he was old enough to drive, though his parents had not said they would allow him to have one. If he put three-quarters of his earnings into a family vacation fund, it would delay the acquisition of a motorcycle considerably.

Barney swallowed hard, considering the matter. "What about Nick?" he asked, stalling. "He isn't making enough to help, is he? Even if he gave the whole paycheck, walking a dog isn't worth much."

"I'll put in my seventy-five per cent, the same as Charles and Molly," Nick said at once. He wanted and needed some new running shoes, but maybe somebody would get him a pair for his birthday—his grandmother was very good at such things if you dropped a hint or two—and he really wanted to go to Disneyland.

"Disneyland is for little kids like Winnie," Barney said.

"Sam went," Nick said. Sam Jankowski was his best friend. "The whole family loved it."

"It isn't just for kids, anyway," Molly said. "I read that more than half the people who go there are grown-ups. Don't be so tight, Barney. Put in your share."

Barney flushed. The whole family kidded him about the way he hung onto his money. He didn't waste it on Cokes and hamburgers or pizza—if he was hungry he ate at home—and he fixed things rather than replaced them, if replacement meant putting out his own funds. "Well," he said reluctantly, "I guess I can contribute, too."

"Seventy-five per cent?" Charles asked, grinning a little.

And Barney had had to nod, yes.

So it had been agreed. They would each put a regular portion of their pay into the cookie jar set aside for that purpose. And if they could save enough to pay for the gas, they'd use the last two weeks of the summer—if Dad had the painting and the roof finished—to go to Disney-land.

Barney made fun of Nick's dog-walking job, but Nick felt lucky to have found any way at all to earn money during the summer. He'd just about given up before he heard about Rudy.

He hated being the smallest boy in the sixth grade. For that matter, a lot of the girls were taller than he was. His mother said that was only natural at his age, because the boys didn't have their growth spurt until later than the girls. Nick still hated it, and it kept him from getting jobs.

Barney made fun of his friendship with Sam, too, because Sam was the *biggest* kid in the class. He was bigger than some of the boys who were in ninth grade.

"You look so funny together," Barney would say. "He's so big, and you're so little. A giant and a midget."

Nick had all he could do to keep from hitting his brother in the mouth when he said things like that. The only reason he didn't do it was that Barney was not only older, he was taller and stronger. He was always trying to provoke Nick into a fight; if Nick struck the first blow, Barney could say, "He started it, so I had to hit him back, didn't I?"

Once their mother happened to overhear an exchange about Sam and came to stand in the doorway of their room. "Barney, I don't want you to say things like that. A giant and a midget. Nick's not a midget, he's just growing slowly right now. Even if he were a midget, it would be a terribly cruel thing to say, to criticize anyone for his size, large or small. People can't help what size they grow to be."

After she'd left—and Barney peeked into the hallway to make sure she'd gone downstairs—Barney's lip curled in derision. "I still think you look funny together, you and that overgrown lunk. Why don't you find a buddy your own size."

Nick refrained from pointing out that if he picked someone his own size it would have to be a fifth grader. "I like Sam," he told his brother coolly. "Which is more than I can say about you." And on that note he left the bedroom he had to share with Barney and went downstairs, too, just so he wouldn't have to listen to his brother any more.

He'd sure be glad when Charles went away to college

and freed a room so the two of them wouldn't have to share anymore. Then he wouldn't have to hear what Barney thought about Sam, or dog-walking jobs, or anything.

As soon as he got home from Mr. Haggard's, he went downstairs and asked Dad about the flashlight, so if that light kept going out in the entry hall of the Hillsdale Apartments he wouldn't have to walk into the pitch dark every night when he brought Rudy home.

It wasn't that he was afraid of the dark, of course. It would just make it easier to get the keys in the locks, if he could see what he was doing.

2

N I C K had started his Rudy-walking job with Mr. Haggard right after school was out. It didn't pay as much as he would have liked to make, especially now with seventy-five per cent going to the Disneyland Fund. But it was better than nothing. The Monday after the third light bulb burned out in the hall, however, things began to look up. Mr. Haggard reported to him when he came in that morning that two other tenants in the building were interested in his services. So after he had taken Rudy for his morning gallop, he went to find out about the new jobs.

Mrs. Helen Sylvan had apartment two, across the hall from Mr. Haggard's. It was identified by the same means as all the others in the place, with a scrawled numeral in black crayon on the brown painted door. Mrs. Sylvan also had a neat white card with her name on it, tacked below the crayon writing.

Mrs. Sylvan was tall and skinny. Even her voice was thin and high-pitched. She had a cat named Eloise, a big white Persian that looked as if she were washed and brushed every day.

Nick glanced around. The place was smaller than Mr. Haggard's, and much fancier. There were knick-knacks on white painted shelves—all kinds of little animal and human figures made of glass and wood and china—and crocheted doilies on everything. It was neat and orderly, with no books or papers lying around. The furniture was polished and there was no dust, though the sofa and chairs didn't look as comfortable as the ones in Mr. Haggard's place.

"I wouldn't trust Eloise to anyone who didn't love animals," Mrs. Sylvan said. "She's very sensitive to things like that. She would know if you didn't like her."

Nick glanced at the cat, who regarded him with wide, unblinking blue eyes. "I like dogs and cats," he assured her, looking back at Mrs. Sylvan. "That's about the only animals I've been around. I think I saw Eloise the other day, when I was walking in the back alley." He didn't mention that Rudy had nearly jerked him off his feet, lunging for the cat, and that he still had black and blue marks on his shins where he'd been dragged into a pile of garbage cans.

Mrs. Sylvan's lips stretched out thin. "She got out when Mr. Griesner came in to fix a leaking faucet. He doesn't care for animals, and he's careless. Whenever you come in or out, you must take care that Eloise doesn't escape. She's too valuable to be loose outside where she's in danger from cars and dogs."

"Yes, ma'am," Nick said.

"She has medicine to take three times a day." She showed him the bottle and the eyedropper. "I'll give her the morning dose before I leave. I'm a bookkeeper at

Capland's Department Store, downtown. I work on a shift where I start late and leave late, and sometimes I stop off to visit with my sister on the way home. But I can give Eloise her last dose before I go to bed. What I need is someone to come in in the afternoon, or even very early in the evening, to give the middle dose. You can start today."

That didn't sound too bad a chore. After a few more instructions Nick put her key on the ring with Mr. Haggard's keys and went on upstairs to apartment three.

There was loud music playing, the kind that Barney liked and Nick hated, so they were always fighting over Barney's radio being on. Sometimes Nick suspected that his brother didn't really like that music, either, but was playing it mostly to annoy Nick.

Behind him, from the foot of the stairs, Mr. Griesner, the apartment manager, yelled so that Nick jumped and spun around.

"Turn that darned stereo down!"

The music went on, unabated, and Nick cleared his throat. "I don't think they heard you, sir."

Mr. Griesner's hair was a gray wiry brush atop his head, touched with various colors where the light came through the colored windows around the front door, so that it was tinted pink and blue and a soft green. On anybody else it might have evoked amusement, but Mr. Griesner was a rather hostile man, Nick had decided. Nothing about him was funny.

"Well, bang on their door and tell them to cool it, will you? Fool hippies, they must be deaf, and they'll make all the rest of us that way, too. I told Mr. Hale we don't need no hippies in this place, but he says anybody can pay the rent, let 'em in. Well, rent or no rent, they can't play music that makes my ears hurt from clear down here. You bang on their door and tell 'em."

"Yes, sir," Nick said, though he didn't see why he should have to confront the hippies. After all, nobody was paying him to be manager of the apartments.

He crossed the upper hall and tapped on the door behind which the music throbbed and crashed. It would be a miracle if they heard his knock over the music. These tenants must be new; he was sure Mr. Haggard had told him, when he first started walking Rudy, that the house was filled with elderly people.

The door swung open. "Yeah? What you selling, kid?"

"Nothing," Nick said. "Mr. Griesner said to tell you the music is too loud. Sir."

He didn't know if the young man was a hippie or not. He did have rather long hair, and he wore blue jeans that Nick's mother would have thrown in the rag bag and tennis shoes with his sockless toes showing through, but he was clean and he smelled of nothing worse than turpentine. There were paint smudges on his T-shirt.

"Oh. Hey, Roy, turn down the stereo," he yelled over his shoulder. Then he grinned at Nick. "You live here, kid? I didn't know there was anybody your age around."

Nick explained about his pet care activities, and the young man nodded. "I noticed all the dogs and cats. We're thinking about getting a pet of some kind, but so far there's only Roy and me. I'm Clyde. He's Roy."

The apartment appeared to be one gigantic room, with a kitchenette at one end of it. Intrigued, Nick stood in the open doorway. There was no real furniture, only a couple of beanbag chairs and some pillows and two mattresses with sleeping bags on them. But there were paintings.

The music had softened, though it still reverberated so that Nick could feel the beat of the bass through the soles of his feet. "You're artists," he said, craning his neck to see the big canvas at the end of the room.

"I'm an artist," Clyde admitted. "Roy's a musician."

Roy had long hair, too—dark instead of blond—that was tied back in a ponytail with a red rag. His jeans were even worse than Clyde's and he wasn't wearing any shoes at all. He nodded at Nick, more engrossed in his guitar than interested in meeting anyone. Nick wondered how he could play his guitar and hear it over the stereo.

"You like painting?" Clyde asked.

"Uh, yes, sometimes," Nick admitted. The big canvas was a glorious splash of color, though Nick couldn't quite make out what it represented.

Apparently Clyde was used to that sort of reception to his work. "It's a sunrise," he offered. "Or a sunset. I haven't decided yet."

Without looking up, Roy said, "Looks like Jacobsmeyer's Drug Store to me." And then, as Nick hesitated, wondering if his leg were being pulled, Roy added, "The night it burned down. Fire, man. Fire. We were living above it at the time, which is one reason we don't have much furniture."

It was rather interesting, but Nick remembered he was supposed to be taking on a new job. "Uh, thanks for turning down the stereo," he said. "I have to go. I'll see you."

"See you," Clyde echoed. Roy didn't look up from his guitar.

When the door closed, Nick went on across the hall to talk to Mrs. Monihan, hoping that Mr. Griesner would be satisfied with the reduction in volume, though the music was still pretty loud.

Mrs. Monihan was the opposite of Mrs. Sylvan in almost every way, except that they both liked animals. She was short and plump, with a round face and a pale blue rinse on her white curls. Every time Nick had seen her, she'd been smiling, as she was now.

"Come in, come in. I have my tickets, I'll be leaving tomorrow." She had been baking, and the apartment was fragrant with the scent of spices. "I can't tell you how much I appreciate your taking care of Maynard and Fred. I couldn't have gone to visit my sister otherwise. I haven't been back to Chicago in twenty-five years, can you imagine? Viola visisted me here once, about ten years back, but I haven't been anywhere. I'm so excited!"

Her apartment was bigger than Mrs. Sylvan's or Mr. Haggard's, and in some ways it was nicer than either of the others. It was neat, though not so much so that a person felt uncomfortable in it. There were books in the bookcases, papers neatly folded on the coffee table, and a plate of cookies set out for him.

"Help yourself," she said. "They're oatmeal-spice, with raisins."

Nick bit into one appreciatively, sinking onto the couch next to Fred. Fred was a cat, too; but he didn't resemble Eloise in the slightest. He was gray-and-white striped, and big; where Eloise was half fur, Fred was mostly cat. He rubbed against Nick's leg and purred when Nick stroked him.

"I've been thinking," Mrs. Monihan said now, regarding him through her glasses. "I'm going to be gone a whole month. That's an awful long time to leave Maynard and Fred here alone all the time. I mean, even with you coming in a couple of times a day to see to their food and water, and taking Maynard outside a bit, they'll get terribly lonesome. So I wondered, if maybe you couldn't stay here?"

Nick strangled on a cookie crumb. When he'd stopped coughing, he said, "What?"

She leaned toward him, then reached up to adjust her hearing aid. "I'm sorry, I forgot to turn it back up again. When those young men had that music on so loud, I turned it off. What was it you said, dear?"

"I said, what did you want me to do?"

"Stay here. Sleep here, in the apartment. Not every night, but once in a while. Maybe two or three nights a week. It would mean so much to Fred and Maynard to have company. There's plenty of food for late night snacks. You could just come up after you walk Rudy."

"I don't know," Nick said slowly. "I'm not sure my folks would let me."

She looked so disappointed he almost relented and agreed to do it, though he didn't really want to And probably his mother wouldn't allow it anyway.

"Would you ask, dear? I'd pay you extra, of course. Couldn't expect you to do it for nothing. Say, double the amount we agreed on for the other things you'll be doing if you'll stay two or three nights a week."

Double. Nick considered that, chewing his second cookie. Gosh, that would make quite a difference in how much he could contribute to the Disneyland fund. And if he kept really busy over here, he wouldn't have to help Dad paint the house.

Nick liked his father very much, and he knew he was an excellent teacher; all the other kids liked him, too. Only he wasn't very mechanical, nor good with his hands; the only other time he'd painted anything, that Nick could remember, was two years ago at his grand-parents' farm, when Mr. Reed had painted the chicken house. Grandma had muttered under her breath that if she'd known he was going to make such a production out of it, she'd have been tempted to get rid of the chickens, instead.

"I don't know. I'll have to ask," Nick told Mrs. Moni-han now.

"Oh, I do hope they'll give you permission. It isn't," she said earnestly, "as if you'd be alone in the house, or anything like that. Those young men are just across the hall—you can tell when they're home because you can hear the music—and there is Mrs. Sylvan downstairs, and Mr. Haggard, and Mr. Griesner is at the back of the house. You can tell your parents that."

He didn't get around to discussing the matter at home right away, though, because when he arrived there a short time later the place was a scene of chaos.

The front door stood wide open, and Winnie was looking out, eating a peanut butter and jelly sandwich, from which the filling oozed down her arm. Beyond her, the telephone was ringing, and the two little boys that Molly took care of were jumping up and down on the couch, squealing. His mother was shouting something down from upstairs. What was she doing home?

Winnie stepped aside so that Nick could enter, paus-ing to lick a glob of jelly off her wrist. Through the dining room windows Nick saw that yellow paint had been spilled on the tarp covering the bushes next to the house, and there was nobody on the ladder. When he moved a little, he saw the paint can lying on its side with a yellow puddle around it on the cement.

"What's going on?" Nick demanded, and moved out of the way when his sister Molly raced in to take the children off the couch and his mother ran into the kitchen to answer the phone. He heard her say, "We don't know yet how bad it is. We're heading for the hospital now."

"Hey, Winnie! Is it Dad? Did he fall off the ladder or something?"

Winnie shook her head. "No, Daddy's not hurt. Well, he did come down the ladder so fast he spilled the paint, and he hit the corner of the house and skinned his elbow, but he's all right."

Dad said when Winnie grew up she was going to be a real beauty. Right now she looked the same as all the rest of the Reeds: straight dark hair, big brown eyes, and a sprinkling of freckles across her nose. Nick had wondered how his father knew what she was going to look like when she grew up until he saw a picture of his mother when she was eight years old. Ah, Winnie was going to look the way his mother did now, that's what Dad had meant. And since Winnie was a girl, it wouldn't matter so much if she didn't get very tall.

"What's going on then?" Nick asked her now, and had to wait until she'd swallowed a bite of the sandwich.

"It's Grandma Tate," she explained. "She fell down the stairs at home, and they think she's got a broken hip."

"Oh, wow. Broken hips are terrible for old people. What're you doing here with the monsters?" he demanded of Molly as she herded the two little boys out of the living room toward him.

"I came when I heard about Grandma, and I had to bring them with me. Nick, see what you can do about that spilled paint, will you? I'm going on back over to the Franklins'; that house is used to these kids' wild ways, and this one isn't. You and Dad ready to go, Mom?"

"Yes. I don't know how long we'll be at the hospital; until they get the x-rays and tell us what's going to happen, I suppose. Nick, dear, Charles is working, and Molly won't be home until after six, so see to something to eat for lunch, all right? Oh, and call Mr. Sundling and tell him I won't be back to work today."

Mrs. Reed worked in an office downtown, and the rest of the family were used to doing for themselves when she wasn't around. After she and Mr. Reed left, and Molly had taken the Franklin kids home, Nick put out bread and cold meat and peanut butter, and he and Winnie, and Barney, when he came home, helped themselves.

Barney had a couple of lawn cutting jobs that afternoon, so after lunch Nick did the best he could with the mess in the patio. It took him quite a while to get things cleaned up, and then, for lack of anything better to do, he did a little painting himself. He didn't mind doing something like that when the whole family wasn't around to tell him he was doing it wrong. He could have gone to see Sam, of course, but he didn't want to leave Winnie alone, and besides he wanted to wait and hear about Grandma.

Mrs. Reed didn't call back until late in the afternoon. Grandma was still being operated on, she said, so she and

Mr. Reed would be having dinner at the hospital. Nick opened a can of soup for Barney and Winnie and himself and made toasted cheese sandwiches to go with it. There was chocolate pudding in the refrigerator, and after they'd each had a dish, they decided that since there wouldn't be enough left to go around tomorrow when the whole family would be home, they might as well have another bowl.

Nick felt comfortably stuffed as he headed back toward Hillsdale Street. He hoped Rudy would be content to walk instead of run, at least until Nick's supper had settled.

There was a U-Haul truck in front of the house next door, and Nick slowed to watch with interest. Somebody was moving in, he saw at once, a family with a girl about his own age and a boy about ten. The whole family was carrying boxes except the boy, who was hauling coiled garden hoses around the side of the house. It was almost a twin to 1230 except that it had been more recently painted and didn't have as much fancy colored glass in the windows.

The girl turned from the truck with a box labeled *Books* just as Nick came abreast. She was small and slim, with dark hair that blew loose around her shoulders. She was wearing a blue and white striped shirt and blue shorts, with blue and white running shoes like his own, except hers weren't falling apart.

She hesitated for only a few seconds, then gave him a faint smile and went on toward the house.

Cute, Nick thought. Why hadn't he had nerve enough to speak to her? Say hi, anyway, and maybe find out her name. Barney would have found out her name.

He kicked a pop can off the sidewalk, then picked it

up to throw in the trash. Shoot, he wasn't ever going to be much like Barney. Actually, he didn't want to be, even if Barney could talk to girls.

As Nick turned onto the walk to the Hillsdale Apartments, the boy next door called out, "Melody, where am I supposed to put this junk?"

"Leave the hose at the side of the house," the girl said, "right by the outside faucet. Put the toolbox around in the garage, I guess. Oh, and Dickie, Dad said to get those empty boxes out of the way. Stack them in the alley for now."

Melody, Nick thought, going up the steps. What a pretty name. He said it again to himself as he unlocked the front door. Melody.

Rudy heard him coming and whined behind the door of apartment one, but that wasn't where he was going, yet. First he had to give Eloise her medicine. He found the key to Mrs. Sylvan's door and let himself in.

Eloise was lying on the sofa. She lifted her head to gaze at him with enigmatic eyes. Nick liked that word. It seemed to him that everybody had enigmatic eyes; you couldn't tell what they were thinking, most of the time. Maybe it was just as well, if they were all thinking what a shrimp he was.

"Hi, Eloise," he said. She didn't blink or move. "Time for your medicine," he told her, and got the bottle and the dropper.

Eloise stayed where she was until he approached within a foot or so of her, and then she suddenly shot past him with a decidedly unfriendly sound.

"Hey, come on. You're supposed to take this stuff so you'll get over whatever's wrong with you. Come on, Eloise. It's important." He didn't feel self-conscious about talking to animals. His Grandma Reed, who lived on a farm, talked to animals all the time. If she could do it, so could he.

Only Eloise wasn't particularly receptive to his small talk. He stalked her through the unnaturally neat apartment, speaking gently all the time, until he cornered her in the bathroom. Maybe this wasn't going to be as easy as he'd thought.

All he had to do was hold her still, get the dropper full of the medicine, and squirt it into her mouth. Only he had a devil of a time catching her, and she scratched him. Luckily he'd had sense enough to close the door, and the bathroom was too small for her to get far away from him. This time he got a towel and wrapped her in it; she didn't like it, but she was a lot smaller than Rudy and he managed to subdue her inside the wrappings. Then he had to pry her mouth open with his fingers while holding her tight against him with that same arm, and used the other hand to administer the medicine with the eyedropper.

"There, that wasn't so bad, was it?" He loosened his grip on the towel and the indignant cat shot away from him, snarling her fury. Nick wondered uneasily how much harder it would be to administer the stuff the next time. Maybe he'd see if Sam would come over and help him.

"I sure hope you get well soon," Nick told the cat as he opened the bathroom door and saw her streak past him to hide under a chair in the living room. "If I'd known how hard this was going to be, I'd have asked for twice as much money to do it."

Eloise glowered at him. He decided to ignore her. He washed off the scratch and put an antiseptic on it from the medicine chest. It wasn't bleeding enough so that he felt the need of a Band-Aid over it.

"See you next time, I guess," he said to the cat as he headed for the door. And that was where he made his mistake.

He turned his back on Eloise and opened the door into the hallway, and the next thing he knew a big white puff of fur ran between his legs, nearly knocking him down, and Eloise disappeared.

He was so busy trying to keep from braining himself by falling against the door jamb that he didn't even see which way she went.

Breathing through his mouth, Nick stood in the dim hallway, listening. He didn't hear a thing. He'd told Mrs. Sylvan that he liked cats, but he was beginning to think that in Eloise's case he might make an exception.

Which way had she gone? Not outside, she had to be trapped in the house because the front door was closed, but it was a big house.

Nick walked toward the rear of the place until he came to the manager's apartment. Behind the door he could hear the television—a ball game. There was no way Nick could see that the cat could have gotten in there, nor found a way directly outside, so he retraced his steps.

In Mr. Haggard's apartment, Rudy whined again, recognizing him. "Be back in a while, boy," Nick called, and looked up the stairs. Eloise could be up there, or she could have hidden in one of the dark corners down here. The light was on again, but the illumination didn't extend to the area beneath the stairs. What was that, a closet under there?

The door was closed, a door painted the same dull

brown as the paneling that ran around the bottom four feet of the walls below the faded wallpaper, so it didn't seem likely the cat could have gotten into the closet. Still, the door didn't fit well at the bottom. Nick tried the door to see, and it came open easily.

No sign of Eloise, though the crowded little cubby-hole was full of plenty of other stuff. Old paint cans, boxes labeled CHRISTMAS ORNAMENTS and INCOME TAX RECORDS, 1969 TO 1975. There was a faint smell that made Nick frown and reach for the small red can in one corner.

Gasoline? Would anybody be crazy enough to store a can of gas in a closet with a bunch of flammable stuff?

He hesitated. It wasn't his house, after all, but it seemed stupid to ask for trouble. He'd mention it to Mr. Haggard, and *he* could bring it up with Mr. Griesner.

And he still hadn't found Eloise.

He started up the stairs, slowly, braced to make a grab if the cat tried to go past him. What was he going to tell Mrs. Sylvan if he couldn't get her cat back into the apartment?

The upper hall was dim, too, though it wasn't even starting to get dark outside yet. And quiet, very quiet. Clyde and Roy must not be home. Mrs. Monihan should still be here, she wasn't leaving until tomorrow. Did he dare ask her assistance in finding Eloise?

What would she think about leaving her own pets, though, in the hands of someone who'd lost a cat the first time he had anything to do with it?

Behind him, there was a scratching sound as a key turned in the lock, and one of the double doors opened inward.

At the same moment, as Nick looked down to see an unfamiliar figure enter the hallway, Eloise practically flew past him and out the front door before the man could close it.

Nick swallowed in despair. What did he do now?

3

THE man was middle-aged and wearing a business suit open to show his paunch with a gold chain across it. Nick thought if he had a belly that stuck out that way, he wouldn't call attention to it with a fancy gold chain. The man looked a him with surprised pale eyes. "What the devil was that?" he asked.

"Mrs. Sylvan's cat. Eloise." Nick ran down the steps and peered out the door. "Did you see which way she went?"

"I didn't even see enough to know it was a cat. Who're you?"

It sounded rude because of the brusque tone. Nick told him, however, very politely. "I'm walking the dog for Mr. Haggard, and taking care of Mrs. Sylvan's and Mrs. Monihan's pets for a few weeks. Excuse me, I have to try to find Eloise."

The man didn't introduce himself, but he had a key, so Nick assumed he had a right to be there. Nick went out and down the steps, trying not to panic. What if

Eloise got run over, or treed by a dog, or just ran away and never came back?

He stood on the front sidewalk, looking in every direction. That big white ball of fur ought to stand out against green lawns and rhododendron bushes, but he didn't see her.

The U-Haul truck was still being unloaded next door. Melody emerged from it with a stack of velvet pillows, and Nick strode toward her, having a perfectly good excuse to talk to her now.

"Have you seen a cat? A big white Persian?"

The girl paused, hugging the cushions to her chest. "Came out of that house a few minutes ago? I thought someone was chasing her, she ran so fast."

"I was, or trying to. Which way did she go?"

Melody gestured between the houses. "Back toward the alley." Was there interest in her face? "I'm Melody Jamison. Do you live next door?"

He explained about his jobs, and then about Eloise. "I have to catch her before Mrs. Sylvan comes home, or I'll probably be fired."

"Wait a minute, and I'll help you," she offered, and ran off to put the pillows on the porch. She led the way through the space between the two houses, apologizing for the mess. "We have to take the truck back first thing in the morning, so we're trying to get everything out tonight. There isn't time to unpack and put everything in place, though, so a lot of it's going into the garage. There! Isn't that her, up there?"

They'd reached the alley, and Melody pointed upward toward the back of 1230. The house was only one story high at the very rear of the building, where an old garage too small to house anything but the smallest of cars jutted to the very edge of the lot. Mr. Griesner had his apartment back here, with a door opening into the yard, and there was an outdoor stairway that climbed the side of the building, crossed the roof of the garage, and then climbed even more steeply to another door that must open into Mrs. Monihan's kitchen. At the very top, on the railing, Eloise sat washing her face.

"Confounded cat. I've got to catch her," Nick said. "I'm not sure how, though. She didn't like me before I gave her the medicine, and now she hates me." He didn't add that the feeling was mutual.

"Maybe I can do it. I'm usually good with cats," Melody said. Up close he saw that her eyes were hazel, and she had a few freckles like his own. "Let me try, OK?"

"Be careful. She scratches," Nick warned.

Melody began, very slowly, to climb the stairs up the side of the house. There was no way Nick could block off every avenue of escape, since if Eloise leaped onto the garage roof she could jump off that in any direction in perfect safety. Nick couldn't cover all the possibilities.

When Melody reached the landing, over the flat part of the garage roof, Eloise ceased licking her paw and watched suspiciously. She hunched down as if preparing to spring, and Melody stopped and began to speak in a soft, coaxing tone. "Pretty kitty. Nice girl. Nice kitty."

Eloise's head swiveled, the unwinking eyes fixing on Nick where he watched below.

Melody spoke without turning around. "Maybe if you got out of her sight, she wouldn't be so tense and she'd let me walk up the rest of the steps."

It would be fine with him if he never saw the cat again, Nick thought, only he was stuck for now. He stepped closer to the building, out of the cat's sight between a pair of garbage cans, expecting that any minute Eloise would leap over his head and take off down the alley.

She didn't, though. A moment later Melody called, "I've got her!" and then her feet sounded on the steps, coming down.

She held Eloise in a reassuringly secure grip. "Maybe I could take her back to wherever she belongs? So you don't upset her again?"

"Sure, fine with me," Nick agreed. When he spoke, Eloise spat at him. "Boy, I don't know how I'm going to keep on giving her medicine if she's going to act like this."

As long as he kept his distance, Eloise seemed content to be carried by someone else. They walked back between the houses toward the front, where there was a new Cadillac parked behind the U-Haul van. Nick vaguely remembered seeing it when he'd come out earlier; it must belong to the man who'd allowed the cat to escape.

Sure enough, the man was coming out onto the porch now, and Mr. Griesner was with him. The stranger carried a white envelope in one hand, and Nick suddenly guessed who he was. Mr. Hale, who owned the apartment house. All the tenants paid Mr. Griesner, who then handed the checks over to the owner.

His guess was verified when he listened to their parting conversation, standing there on the sidewalk rather than interrupting until the men got out of the way.

"What you want me to do about that linoleum, then?" the manager asked. "Anybody trips over it and gets hurt, I wouldn't bet they wouldn't sue."

34

"Yeah, people sue over anything these days," Mr. Hale said. He ran a hand over his head, smoothing down the thinning strands of gray hair. "Well, tack it down again, and I'll see about getting some new stuff for the whole hall. See if I can find some on sale, maybe."

"I'll tack it down. It's not going to last long, though, it's too wore out," Mr. Griesner said. "What about the painters? You interested in talking to 'em?"

"I want the place painted, I'll find my own painters. You know what they'll do to my taxes if I paint this place? Up they go, every little improvement a man makes. No, better to take care of the stuff inside first, where the assessor won't notice it for a while. They make it hard for a man to make a living on his investments, those tax people. Sometimes I don't think it's worth it, the little a man makes from a rental unit. I'd sell my places like this one, if I could. Trouble is, nobody's got the cash to buy it, and it's practically impossible to get financing on it. Banks want so much interest, people can't afford it. And old places like this, banks don't want to finance, anyway. They expect everything to be up to snuff—plumbing, wiring—like a brand new house." He shook his head at the problems of being a landlord. "Anyway, I'm not going to put any more money into it than I have to. One of these days the recession will be over, and people will have money again. Maybe all the tenants could get together, then, and buy it themselves."

Mr. Griesner made a snorting sound. "Nobody lives in this place is ever going to have enough money to buy anything, even if they all went together."

Nick wondered if his father knew about the relationship between painting and taxes. He glanced at the

Cadillac and saw Melody looking at it, too. It was out of place in this neighborhood of Fords, Chevies, and Volkswagens.

"Well," Mr. Hale said, "see you next month. And don't take any excuses about late rent from those hippies, you hear? It's not our fault they don't work steady. They either pay on time, or out they go."

"I didn't want to let 'em in in the first place," Mr. Griesner said morosely. "Play that music loud enough to break a man's eardrums. Can I tell Mrs. Sylvan you're planning to replace that linoleum, then, and these repairs I make are just temporary, till you can do it?"

Mr. Hale waved the envelope in one pudgy hand. "Yes, yes, tell her we're taking care of it. Ah, caught the cat, did you?"

He smiled, coming down the steps, passing between them to get into the Cadillac. Nick and Melody went up to the front door, which the manager had not yet locked, waiting for them to enter. He muttered more to himself than to the two youngsters, "Anything doesn't get done, it's always my fault; I'm the one they complain to."

He swung the door shut behind them and turned the button that locked it. "Watch the floor there, foot of the stairs. Worn place, you can catch a toe."

"We just have to put Eloise back in the apartment," Nick said. He was glad when the Persian had been dumped inside and the door secured behind her. "Thanks for helping," he told Melody Jamison. "Now I don't have to worry about her until tomorrow, and I'll be more careful about keeping her shut in then. I wonder how much sicker she'll get if I can't manage to get that medicine into her when I'm supposed to."

36

Melody grinned. "She doesn't seem very sick. Well, Daddy will be wondering where I disappeared to. I'll see you later, Nick."

Nick went on upstairs after she'd gone, to get his final instructions from Mrs. Monihan about taking care of Fred and Maynard.

"It's nothing difficult," the old lady assured him. She showed him their dishes—Fred's was orange and Maynard's was yellow—and where she kept the food. "Fred has some of the dry stuff in his dish all the time, and every evening I give him half a can of this other. If he doesn't eat it at once, you might as well let Maynard have it, because Fred will only eat it fresh. And this, in the big bag, is Maynard's food. It says to mix it with water, but I don't, ever. He eats it dry, and then drinks a lot of water afterward, so you always keep his water dish filled. That's the blue one. Would you like to walk Maynard now, just to see how the two of you get along?"

"Sure," Nick agreed. He wondered what Rudy would think, when his walking companion kept going in and out with every animal but himself. He was certain Rudy knew about Eloise and would know about Maynard, too.

Maynard was about the same size as Eloise and looked sort of like a once-white mop in need of a good bleaching. His eyes were like little brown buttons peeking out through the shaggy hair, bright and inquisitive and friendly. When he wagged his tail, his whole rear end moved.

"Come on, Maynard," Nick said, and snapped the leash onto the red collar.

Walking Maynard was a tame experience after Rudy.

Maynard tugged and rushed, too, but since he weighed only about twelve pounds instead of eighty-five, he couldn't go anywhere Nick didn't want him to go. He was willing to run when Nick ran, which he did at Nick's side instead of dragging him along behind.

Nick took him down the alley, the way Mr. Haggard had suggested he start out each of Rudy's excursions. "Take care of business there, so he won't embarrass you on somebody's lawn," the old man had said, and it worked just as well for the smaller dog.

When he got back, Mrs. Monihan gave him another of the cookies, and said she'd leave the rest in the cookie jar for him while she was gone. Nick hesitated. "Is Fred an escape artist? Do I have to be careful about him getting away?"

"Oh, my no! Fred can take care of himself. I leave that kitchen window open most nice days, and he goes in and out by himself, up and down the back stairs, you know. I don't ever leave that door unlocked, of course, unless I sit out there and take the sunshine for a bit. I wouldn't want anybody to get in that way. Well, I know you're going to take good care of my family while I'm gone, so I won't worry about them. I've left my sister's address and phone number on the pad there, just in case, though. Did you ask your mother about staying overnight sometimes?"

Nick explained about the problem at home and why he hadn't asked. And then, almost without meaning to, he said, "I'll do my best to talk her into it. I think maybe she'll let me, when she knows I won't be alone in the building."

Mrs. Monihan smiled and looked relieved. "I'm sure

I'm leaving Fred and Maynard in good hands And I know you'll do the best you can."

They said goodby then, and Nick left. The minute he set foot in the hall, he could have kicked himself. Why had he told Mrs. Monihan he'd try to talk his mother into letting him stay over sometimes in her apartment? That was the last thing he wanted to do, even if her cookies were good. Oh, well, if it worked out, at least it would get him away from Barney for a night or two a week. There was that bright side to it. And what could happen? The place was full of people.

Rudy was the last one to receive attention, and Nick could tell by the way he acted that he'd known Nick was in the house and didn't understand why he'd had to wait for his exercise.

The big black-and-tan dog leaped on him until Nick commanded him sharply to sit, then sank back on his haunches and let his tongue hang out. He looked for all the world as if he were grinning with pleasure that Nick had finally arrived.

Mr. Haggard was huddled in his usual chair, watching television instead of reading. He looked more shrunken up than usual.

"Is there anything I can do for you before we leave?" Nick asked. It hurt the old man to move around much, so Nick had fallen into the habit of bringing him things.

"No, thanks, boy. Unless . . . well, maybe my pain pills. They're on the counter."

Nick brought the little prescription bottle and a glass of water. "You feeling worse, Mr. Haggard?"

"Not feeling very good," the old man admitted. "Have a nice walk now."

It was a good walk. Mr. Haggard didn't care where they went, as long as Rudy was exercised for at least an hour, twice a day. But tonight Nick was so worn out with everything that had happened that instead of going to the park, or wandering very far, he just stayed in the neighborhood. And part of the time, he watched Melody and her family finish unloading the U-Haul. He didn't talk to her anymore though.

Nobody even noticed when Nick came home. The car was in the driveway, the hood still warm, and he remembered then that his parents had been at the hospital.

Winnie was in bed, but everybody else was in the dining room eating hamburgers. Sometimes someone called in an order at the drive-in and then failed to pick it up, and Charles got the food at half price and brought it home for a late snack.

Tonight there were cheeseburgers and pineapple milkshakes, and french fried onion rings. Barney sipped through a thick straw and grimaced. "Pineapple! Whatever happened to chocolate shakes?"

"You come over and pay for it, you can have any flavor you want," Charles told him. "You want a shake, Nick?"

He was, he realized, starving. He helped himself and looked to his mother, who wasn't eating but simply seemed to have collapsed into a chair in exhaustion.

"How's Grandma, Mom?"

"Her hip is fractured. They're going to do further surgery tomorrow. They'll have to put a steel pin in it to hold it. Molly, get out a roast and put it on for dinner tomorrow, will you? I expect we'll be there at the hospital for most of the day, until Mother comes out from under the anesthetic and knows we're there and that everything is all right."

"Is she hurting bad?" Nick asked around a mouthful of cheeseburger.

"Well, they've given her something for that, but yes, I think it's very painful. She moans, even now, if she tries to move at all. Oh, my, it's so late. Finish up here, kids, and everybody get on to bed. I'm going up now, I think."

And so, once again, Nick didn't have a chance to discuss the matter of staying all night at the Hillsdale Apartments.

The next morning, he got up and went over to Hillsdale early, thinking maybe he'd get one last chance to see Mrs. Monihan. And maybe somehow he could talk her out of needing someone to stay nights. But by the time he got there, she was already gone. So he fed both Fred and Maynard, and then he and Maynard went for a walk. Later he took Rudy out. Mr. Haggard sent him on a couple of errands, mostly to get some more of his pain pills. Nick thought the old man looked bad. He wondered if he ought to see his doctor. But he didn't ask. After all Mr. Haggard's health was Mr. Haggard's business.

Every time he passed Mrs. Sylvan's door Nick was glad that he didn't have to deal with Eloise until later. Maybe by then she would have forgotten him. He didn't think so, though.

Things at home that day were even more hectic than they had been the day before. And Nick found himself minding Winnie most of the day. Not that he minded.

He liked Winnie. But he had a feeling Barney wasn't cutting grass all day. He could have helped so Nick could have spent some time with Sam.

Later, just after supper, he went back to Hillsdale. Remembering his success with the towel the night before, he started out with the towel, and found it worked pretty well. Eloise didn't like it, but he was a lot happier. And this time he saw to it that she didn't escape. He took care of Fred and Maynard with no trouble. He hadn't even considered spending the night so soon. So that didn't worry him.

Mr. Haggard didn't mind where Nick went with Rudy, or what he did, so that night Nick ran with him over to Sam's house, and then Sam walked back with him after they'd gone all the way around the park. It was dark by the time they headed toward the Hillsdale Apartments.

"After you take Rudy home, let's go back to my house and play Space Invaders," Sam suggested. "My mom made doughnuts this afternoon."

Sam's mother didn't have a job away from home, so she was always making good things to eat. "OK," Nick agreed. "I'll call from your house and make sure it's all right with my mom. If she's even there. My grandma fell yesterday and broke her hip, so my folks have been at the hospital with her most of the time."

"I guess it's tough to break your bones when you're old," Sam said in sympathy. "They don't heal the way kids' bones do." Sam was an expert on broken bones. He'd fractured an arm falling out of a tree and a finger catching a ball without a glove. "Come on, Nick, I'll race you the rest of the way."

Nick won, as he usually did, though Sam wasn't far

behind. He'd have been even closer if Rudy hadn't gotten in his way so that Sam tangled in the leash. Sam was a good sport, though. He didn't complain about Rudy causing him to lose. Sam was a good best friend, Nick thought, and was glad Sam felt the same way about him.

That night when they got back to the Hillsdale Apartments, the light on the porch was on, but the light in the hall was out. Nick told Sam how many times it had happened, and Sam was as puzzled as he was. They both listened closely when Nick opened the front door, but all they could hear was noise from upstairs. In spite of the dark, Clyde and Roy seemed to be having a party. As the two boys came in, the party spilled out into the hall, and the noise was even more deafening.

That reminded Nick of the gas can he had seen the night before, and he told Mr. Haggard about it.

Over the next few days, Sam went with him every evening. He helped with Eloise and Fred and Maynard, too. It almost wasn't like a job, at all, since they raced and talked and enjoyed themselves. Nick wondered if he ought to feel guilty about getting paid for having a good time.

On Friday night they brought Rudy home later than usual; Sam had gotten some birthday money from his grandmother, and he'd treated Nick to a hamburger. After Rudy sat watching them, drooling, Sam sighed and bought a third burger for the dog. "You can't enjoy your own with him watching you that way," he said.

They joked until they got close to Hillsdale and then Sam said, "Hey, what is it about this place? First your

43

hall light is out all the time, and now the streetlight is out."

They approached the corner of Hillsdale and Groves Streets. It wasn't so dark they were in danger of running into the telephone poles at the edge of the sidewalk, but it was enough to make them careful, stepping off the curb to cross the alley.

Rudy, knowing he was close to home and his "cookie" reward, strained against the leash. And then he suddenly plunged into the pitch black alley behind the house, "whuffing" in the same way he had done that time when Nick had wondered if there was someone in the entry hall.

Rudy was so big and so strong that when he veered, anyone trying to hold him veered, too. Sometimes, as now, Nick thought Rudy wasn't even aware that he was dragging anyone with him.

"Hey, what's that?" Sam demanded. They both saw it at the same time, the bright orange tongue of flame brilliant against the blackness at the back of the house.

"Fire!" Nick felt the leash jerked out of his hand as Rudy lunged forward, and he had no choice but to let him go. "Sam, it's fire!"

It was too dark to see—it wasn't until later that they realized the streetlight at the other end of the block was out, too—but Nick had a sense of movement ahead of him, more movement than Rudy's.

He had no time to worry about the dog now. The house was made of wood—old, dry wood—and the trash stacked at the foot of the back wall was on fire. Flames leaped three feet, four, and then twice that high, and he saw that stacks of big cardboard boxes had carried the fire to the edge of the garage roof.

"There's a call box on the corner, across the street," Nick cried. "Ring the alarm, Sam, and then bang on the front door and try to get people out of the house. I'll try to find a hose and turn it on the fire; maybe I can put it out."

He didn't wait to see if Sam followed orders. He just remembered that hose that Dickie Jamison had left beside the house next door, and hoped it was still there. He also wished desperately that he'd brought the flashlight. He stumbled toward the house, fell and scraped his hands on something metallic, then groped along the ground for the hose. Oh, boy, it had to be there, he thought, his mouth dry and his chest aching with fear and exertion. It had to be there.

There was enough light now from the fire to show him the hose, coiled like a great sleeping serpent. Nick was shaking so that he could hardly connect the hose to the faucet. His heart threatened to pound right through his chest wall.

As he felt the gush of water through the plastic hose and tugged the loose end of it back toward the alley, he heard Sam pounding on the door up front and yelling. Behind him, a light went on in the Jamisons' house, and a man's voice called out, "What's going on?"

"Fire," Nick gasped, and ran.

4

T H E flames dipped briefly as the spray from the hose nozzle passed over them, then rose again at once, even higher, as the spray moved on.

Nick's heart was pounding harder than it did when he'd just run a mile, and his hands were so greasy with sweat he could hardly hold the hose. It was such a small stream of water, and already the fire had spread through the stacked up cartons, especially the ones that had contained shredded paper packing material, so that the entire back of the garage seemed ablaze.

He heard someone shouting, and then feet in the gravel of the alley behind him.

"Get another hose," a man yelled, and there were more running feet.

"Call the fire department," someone else said, but already they heard the sirens in the distance. Sam would have turned in the alarm from the box on the corner in front of the house. Dimly Nick was aware of the pounding feet from somewhere nearer by, and excited voices.

"Wet down the edge of the roof," a man beside him said, and Nick recognized Melody Jamison's father. He was carrying a red fire extinguisher, and Nick felt a profound sense of relief that he was no longer totally responsible for whatever was going to happen. "If we can keep that roofing from catching, maybe we can slow it down until the firemen get here."

Obediently, Nick focused the water on the edge of the roof that overhung the garage wall; he saw the logic of Mr. Jamison's idea. The flames still leaped against the wooden wall, but the boxes were burning down a little now, and while the wall might be smoldering, the roof so far was not burning.

Nick lifted his eyes and saw a small figure in the window above, at the top of the outside stairs. Fred sat on the window ledge inside, barely visible in the pinkish light from the fire below.

The thought of Fred and Maynard—and Rudy and Mr. Haggard and even Eloise—being burned to death made him feel sickish. Were there enough people fighting the fire so that he could put down the hose and run inside to make sure the old man and all the pets were safe?

Not Rudy, he remembered suddenly. Rudy had run down the alley, leash dragging behind him, just before the fire exploded into all this light. Nick turned his head and saw Melody Jamison and a woman he assumed was her mother, hugging their bare arms against the night chill, eyes fixed on the fire that, while no longer spreading so rapidly, was still burning brightly.

47

"Here," Nick said, and thrust the hose toward the girl. "Keep playing it on the edge of the roof, your dad said. I've got to get the animals out, just in case." Melody gulped and obeyed.

The sirens were nearer, now; in fact, as Nick ran around the corner of the house he saw flashing red lights and heard the roar of powerful engines. People were coming out of their houses all along the street.

Sam was on the front porch, and the door was open. Mr. Haggard stood inside, his white hair standing up in wisps around his ears in the light that streamed from his apartment behind him.

"The fire department's here, I think it'll be all right," Nick said, out of breath. "It wouldn't hurt to wait outdoors, though. I'm going upstairs to check on Mrs. Monihan's pets. Rudy got away, sir, but I'll find him as soon as the fire's out."

He could smell the smoke very strongly as he raced up the stairs. There was no music and no light under the door where Clyde and Roy lived, and he was shaking so he had trouble getting the key in Mrs. Monihan's lock. Maynard leaped into his arms the minute the door opened, and Fred pressed against him, too.

"Come on, just to play it safe, we'll go outside," Nick told them, and snapped the leash onto the little dog. It was a good thing it was kept on the table just inside the door, or he'd have gone without it.

He glanced briefly toward the back of the building and saw the reddish glow through the kitchen window, so he knew they didn't have the fire under control yet.

Maynard scampered ahead of him on the stairs, while Fred led the way, out into the cool safety of the night. The streetlight was out, as were the downstairs hall and porch lights at 1230, but everybody else in the neighborhood had turned on their outside lights.

It seemed to Nick that a long time had elapsed and he continued to breathe heavily, though it couldn't have been more than ten minutes since they'd seen that first spark in the darkness. Mr. Haggard, leaning on his metal walker, had managed to get down the steps onto the sidewalk, where some of the neighbors stood with him, talking.

Sam was nowhere in sight. He must have gone back to where he could see the fire, Nick thought, and took Maynard on around the house. He hoped Fred was looking out for himself, as Mrs. Monihan had said he could.

There were two fire trucks and about a dozen firemen. Their hoses were a lot bigger than the little garden hoses Nick and the neighbors had used; within minutes, the flames were extinguished, though the firemen continued to play water over the blackened debris, just to make sure.

Mr. Jamison was coiling up his own hose, and he looked at Nick in the light from the fire trucks. "Good thing you moved fast, young fellow," he said. "If that roof had gone up before the firemen got here, they might have lost the house. Not to mention the place *we* just bought." He glanced at the house next door, only a few feet separating the adjoining walls. "I only hope Dickie wasn't in any way responsible for this mess."

"Me? Hey, Dad, I haven't been out of the house since before supper!" Dickie wiped at his nose, leaving a smudge from the soot that had settled there. "And I'm smart enough not to monkey around with matches, anyway."

One of the firemen came toward them, his face rather grim. "Looks like what burned is mostly junk, except for this back wall. They'll have to replace that. Lucky it wasn't a lot worse. Anybody know why there was so much trash back here? Surely the alley isn't always that full of burnable stuff, is it? There's no burning allowed in these alleys, you know. There isn't room to get a barrel far enough from the backs of the houses."

"I don't think anybody was deliberately burning any-thing," Mr. Jamison said. "At least, nobody in my family was. We did haul a lot of packing boxes out here earlier this week. There were too many for the regular garbage collection, but someone was coming for them tomorrow. I had them all stacked behind our own place, until they could be hauled away."

"Some of them were over here," Nick said slowly. It made him nervous, the way the fireman was looking at everybody, and he didn't want to cast suspicion on any-body. But it seemed important to tell everything he knew, in case the fire department could figure out what had actually happened, so it wouldn't happen again. "When the fire went up, I saw the boxes. Stacked up all across the back wall."

The fireman's eyes locked on Nick's. His skin had a reddish tint because of the lights that still flashed on the trucks behind him. "You the one turned in the alarm, son?"

"No, that was my friend Sam." Nick gestured toward him. "We both saw it at the same time, and I knew where the people next door had left their hose, so I ran for that. Sam turned in the alarm and warned the people in the house."

Mr. Griesner's fuzzy head materialized out of the

shadows. "Didn't warn me. I didn't know a thing until I heard the fire trucks. Boy, I don't know what Mr. Hale is going to say about this. He hates to spend money to fix the place up, but he's sure going to have to rebuild that wall."

"You live in the back apartment, sir?"

"Yeah, that's right. I'm the manager," Mr. Griesner said. "My place would have been next to go, after the garage."

"These boys did a good job," Mr. Jamison put in. "Moved fast, did the right things."

"How did the fire start?" the fireman wanted to know. "Anybody see what happened?"

For a moment there was only silence and the small sounds of the drowned fire. The smell was sharp, acrid, and it hurt Nick's nose and throat. He swallowed.

"Sam and I were coming across the end of the alley, there, walking Rudy. He's Mr. Haggard's dog, from apartment one, in the front. We noticed the streetlight was out on the corner, and the one at the end of the next block, too, so the alley was darker than usual. Rudy barked and jerked me sideways and took off down the alley as if he were after something, and we saw the sparks. It was only a minute—seconds, really—before the fire was all over the place."

The fireman—Nick finally recognized him as Mr. Conrad, who sometimes took up the collection in church —was looking at him and Sam in a way that made Nick shift uneasily from one foot to the other. Not as if Nick were being helpful, but as if he were under suspicion!

"You didn't see what caused the sparks?" Mr. Conrad asked.

This time it was Sam who answered. "Just a little

flame, at first, and then a whole lot of fire. We couldn't see what started it."

"And you say the dog barked at something, or someone, in the alley? Did he usually do that? Bark at people, say, if there was someone around?"

"He never barked at anybody before that I know of," Nick said. "Not while I was walking him. Even when we passed other dogs that barked at him, Rudy didn't. He'd chase cats, though," he felt compelled to say. "He could have been after a cat when he pulled away from me. We didn't hear anything."

"No feet on the gravel, nothing like that?"

"No, sir. Not that I noticed."

And then Mr. Conrad said something that made Nick both alarmed and angry, all at once. "You boys didn't start it, did you? Trying out a smoke back here, something like that? Playing with matches?"

Nick was so stunned that for a minute he couldn't reply at all. It was Sam who yelped a protest. "Hey! No, we never did anything like that!"

"Better to admit it now, if you did," Mr. Conrad told them, and he didn't sound friendly the way he did when he greeted Nick's father at church on Sunday mornings. "Because our investigators will be out here to find out what happened. We can't have people setting fires, and we try to find out how every fire got started so we can prevent future ones. I know boys sometimes snitch a few cigarettes and try smoking, and once in a while they drop a match or a cigarette and start a fire when they don't mean to."

"Well, *we* didn't," Sam said, sounding indignant. "My folks would about kill me if I ever did that, and besides, I think it's stupid to smoke. Or play with matches, either. We're not little kids, to do something dumb like that."

Mr. Conrad asked more questions, and he wrote down their names and addresses, which struck them both as ominous. Not that he could prove anything against them, because of course they hadn't done anything wrong, but it was most uncomfortable to be under suspicion.

Finally the firemen turned off the flashing red lights and the neighbors drifted back to their own homes. The Jamisons were among the last to leave.

"I still don't understand how our boxes got over against the back of the house next door," Mr. Jamison said, sounding troubled. "I hope it wasn't because someone moved them just to start a fire in them."

"Why would anyone do that?" Mrs. Jamison asked. She was a pretty woman, looking much like Melody, though now that the trucks had gone it was too dark to see her.

"I don't know. Well, I hope that's the end of the excitement. And I still think you did a fine job," Mr. Jamison told Nick. "A good thing you noticed where Dickie left the hose. Come on, let's go inside; it's too cold out here to stand around in our shirtsleeves."

And so at last only Nick and Sam were left, holding Maynard.

"Criminy," Sam said. "Imagine, blaming us! If we hadn't seen the fire and turned in the alarm, the whole house could have burned down."

"Yeah," Nick agreed. "Listen, Sam, I have to find Rudy. Let's walk through the alley and see if he's down there somewhere."

"What if there's somebody there?" Sam asked. "I

mean, we know *we* didn't start any fire, but somebody did. Either accidentally or on purpose. Nobody ran out of the alley on this end, but somebody could have gone the other way."

"We didn't hear anybody," Nick reminded him. "Nobody could run on the gravel without making some noise."

"Rudy didn't make much noise. I'll bet somebody who was barefooted wouldn't have, either."

"Why would anybody be barefooted, when it's cool enough to wear a jacket?" Nick asked, and then, more slowly, said, "You mean someone deliberately started the fire and was barefoot so he could move quietly? But why would anybody do that, Sam?"

"Why did somebody move the packing boxes from behind the house next door over to this one? They weren't over here when you went through the alley this morning, were they?"

"No. Well, a couple of small ones, but that's all." Nick frowned in the darkness. "Sam, you think somebody really did it on purpose? Not just accidentally?"

It was hard to believe that anybody would do such a thing. Yet Nick knew such things *did* happen. More and more often, when the TV news reported a major fire, the word *arson* came up. And arson meant a fire that was deliberately set.

They began to walk down the alley, and Nick whistled and called "Hey, Rudy! Here, boy! Here, Rudy!"

Maynard trotted along on his little leash; like the bigger dog, he enjoyed poking his nose into the refuse set out for tomorrow's trash collection, but when he tried to go too far in the wrong direction, it was easy to pull him back. Suddenly Maynard whined and tugged Nick to one side, and there was a joyful barking reply.

"It's Rudy! Here, Sam, take Maynard. Where are you, boy? Behind the fence?"

Now Rudy whined and leaped happily against the picket fence; his warm rough tongue licked at Nick's fingers when they were pressed between the boards. Nick groped along, feeling for a gate and not finding one.

"You stupid dog, how'd you get in there?" Perplexed, Nick glanced toward the lighted house set in the middle of the yard. "There are people up, but to get to their door we'd have to go all the way around the block. And they might not like finding out they've got a horse-sized dog in their yard."

"There must be a gate somewhere," Sam said, and joined in the effort to find it. "If he could jump over it to get in, you'd think he could jump over it to get out."

Rudy, however, though he tried to reach them, didn't jump nearly high enough to get over the fence. And if there was a hole where he could have crawled under, Nick couldn't find it.

Finally Sam gave a cry of triumph. "Here's a gate! Only it's locked on the inside. My foot's too big to fit between the boards, and I can't reach the latch. See if you can step in there, Nick, and reach up and unlock it."

Nick's running shoe would fit between the slats in the fence if he forced it. He hoped he wasn't stuck there. He reached up and found the latch, a difficult one to manipulate without seeing it, and then heard the welcome *click* as it gave way.

Rudy bounded out to meet them, knocking Maynard over so that the little mop dog yipped once, then threw himself with delight against his rescuers.

"Down!" Nick commanded sharply. "Sit!"

Rudy sat . . . right on Maynard. This time Maynard ki-yied, and Sam untangled the dogs while Nick got the gate relocked and pried his foot out of the fence. Just as he jerked free, a door opened in the house inside the yard and a man's voice called out, "What's going on out there? Is somebody running through my yard again? Doggone it, I'm going to call the cops if people don't stay out of here! Why you think we lock the gate, if we wanted people in our yard?"

Nick wasn't sure why he felt guilty, but he did. Was that what had happened? Had Rudy chased someone from the scene of the fire and jumped over the fence after him, only to be trapped because he couldn't unlock the gate and didn't find his way out the front?

Rudy's chain dragged across his foot, and he grabbed for the leather loop at the end of it. "Come on, let's get out of here," Nick muttered, and they all turned and ran.

The smell of wet burned wood was a strong reminder of the near catastrophe as they walked back down the alley and to the street. Nick was getting cold, and he zipped his sweatshirt and pulled up the hood, as well. Someday, he thought, he was going to try living in a climate where it stayed warm in the evenings in the summertime, the kind of places Sam talked about. He had lived in Indiana and in Nevada and Texas, before his family moved to Northern California.

His guilt increased when he saw that old Mr. Haggard was still waiting on the front porch. The outside light had once more been replaced, and Mr. Griesner was even now on a ladder, screwing a new bulb into the fixture in the entry hall.

"We found him. Somehow he got inside a yard and couldn't get back out until we unlatched the gate," Nick said. Up close, he saw that the old man's face was deeply creased with fatigue or pain. "I'll come back after I've put Maynard in his apartment and make you some cocoa, shall I?"

"That would be very kind of you," Mr. Haggard said. He smiled, reaching out a hand to Rudy's big head. "I knew you wouldn't let anything happen to him, boy."

It made Nick uncomfortable, because he really had no control over what happened to Rudy. And he still wondered how the big Airedale had gotten behind a locked gate. All the pets in his care were still safe, though. He was sure glad about that.

Fred had returned and followed them into the house. He and Maynard headed for their brightly colored bowls to eat and drink, and Nick locked the door behind them. At Mrs. Sylvan's door he could see a crack of light, so she had come home, too. He was glad the fire hadn't spread so he'd have had to get Eloise out of there; he didn't know how he could have kept her from running away.

It was only after he'd fixed Mr. Haggard's cocoa, and the boys had each shared a cup with him, that they emerged from apartment one, ready to go home. His folks would be wondering why he was so late, and Sam's would, too.

Sam opened the front door, then turned his head. "What are you doing? What's under there?"

For Nick, struck by the memory of that red gas can in the closet under the stairs, had turned back. What if it had been there, and there had been a fire! For a moment he thought the door was locked, for it resisted his effort to open it. And then it gave under his hand, and in the light of the newly installed hall bulb Nick stared into the closet.

The red can was gone. Then Mr. Haggard had done something about it. The old man had been in so much pain lately, it had seemed unlikely to Nick that he would. But the idea of it must have worried him, too.

5

N O B O D Y noticed that Nick was unusually late getting home. He had been spending time with Sam after his evening walk with Rudy, and now everyone just assumed that's where he had been. He wondered if he should tell about the fire. But even if he had really wanted to, everyone was so busy talking that no one would have listened.

Mr. and Mrs. Reed were still spending a lot of time at the hospital. Grandma was better, but she was still uncomfortable. Molly was full of stories about the outrageous things the Franklin kids tried. And Barney, as usual, was eating up a storm.

Nick remembered guiltily that he had never mentioned his chance to make extra money by staying a few nights a week with Fred and Maynard. Mrs. Monihan had been gone now since Tuesday, and he would have to do something about that soon. Fred and Maynard were always glad to see him when he came, but he had never had the sense that they were suffering at being left alone. Still, the extra money did look good. On the other hand, if someone had tried to burn the place down, he'd rather be sleeping at home, in case they tried again. But that would leave Fred and Maynard alone in a burning building, and he didn't like to think of that either.

If it hadn't been for that gas can stored in the front closet—the can that was now gone—and the light bulbs that burned out so readily, it would be easy to believe that the fire in the alley had been started by kids, stupidly fooling around with matches. As it was, Nick felt distinctly uneasy about the entire matter, and he decided he'd really like to talk to his father about it. Only his father looked awfully tired, and went upstairs before there was a chance to say anything.

So Nick tried telling his brother. Barney's half of the room was meticulously neat, compared to Nick's, and he stood in his pajamas, writing in a new page of lawn-mowing dates on the sheet Scotch taped to the closet door.

"And when I looked in the closet again," Nick concluded, after speaking to Barney's back for several minutes, "the gas can was gone."

Barney, finished with his chart, turned and came to sit on the bed opposite Nick's. "Well, you told that old Mr. Haggard about the can being in the closet, didn't you?"

"Yes. It seemed dangerous there."

"So he probably told Mr. Griesner, and *he* took it out and put it in a better place."

Nick hadn't thought of that. Of course, that was logical.

"You didn't smell any gasoline at the scene of the fire, did you?"

Nick tried to remember. "No. I'm sure I'd have noticed if there'd been a smell like gasoline."

"Well, then, it's not very likely anybody poured gas on the boxes to get them going. You wouldn't need to, anyway, because cardboard and packing stuff burns like crazy without any help at all. Besides, the fire department men are trained to look for things like that. If it's arson, they can just about always tell. Why would anybody want to burn down that old dump, anyway?"

"It's not a dump," Nick protested. "It's old, and old-fashioned, and it needs paint and some fixing up, but Dad says most of those old houses were built better than the places they build today, or they wouldn't still be here after a hundred years. But Rudy did bark, and chase after something, off down the alley."

"Probably a cat," Barney said. He slid into bed and twiddled his radio dial, bringing in some of that music Nick hated instead of what had been playing when Nick entered the room. "You said he's wild to chase cats."

"It wasn't a cat that locked him inside that fence."

"He could have chased a cat in there. If he was running and took a jump, he could clear a pretty high fence, couldn't he? And then the cat climbed a tree, or went in the house, or something, and Rudy was stuck in the yard, too dumb to jump back out the way he came in. Come on, Nick, turn out the light. I have to be up early."

"Turn off the radio, then, so I can go to sleep, too."

"I've got it down low," Barney said, and closed his eyes, hands folded on his chest.

Nick considered throwing his fielder's glove at the radio and knocking it off the table. Maybe it would break and stop playing. Only he supposed his parents would expect him to pay for it if he broke it. He turned out the light and hoped the investigator from the fire department would decide that the blaze had simply been an accident. He'd sure feel better about it then.

On Saturday morning, though, when he reached the Hillsdale Apartments, he saw with alarm that there was an ambulance at the curb, along with the Cadillac belonging to Mr. Hale, and another car that, while unmarked, bore an official license plate.

The front door stood open, and the entry hall was full of people. Nick stood looking in, not wanting to push through between them. Mr. Hale was talking, sounding agitated and upset.

"Well, what are you doing to find out who did it?"

A stranger in a checked sport coat and slacks replied more calmly. "We're doing everything we can, sir. At this point there's no reason to think it was an attempt to burn your house. We found a few matches, unlighted ones, scattered along the edge of the alley, behind the house next door. More than likely it was kids fooling around, and when the fire went up, they got scared and ran and threw the rest of the matches. We'll talk to the people on this block, sir, make sure the parents of all youngsters are aware of the situation."

"You don't think the streetlights being out had anything to do with it?" Mr. Hale persisted. "Funny one on each end of the block would go out at the same time, just before the back of my house catches fire."

"We're investigating," the newcomer said smoothly. Then his gaze fell upon Nick. "You live here, young man?"

"Is somebody hurt?" Nick asked, because the ambulance was there, back door open as if the attendants were here, inside the house.

"Old man is sick, I guess," Mr. Hale said. "Apartment one. Fire was too much for him."

"Mr. Haggard?" Nick stepped inside, now able to see that the door was open into the front apartment. "What happened? He was all right when I was here last night!"

"You were here last night? Were you here the time of the fire?" the investigator said, but Nick was already moving past him.

"Mr. Haggard! Mr. Haggard, what happened?" Nick demanded. Nobody stopped him from going inside, and the two men easing the old fellow onto the wheeled cart turned to look at him.

"You a relative?" one of them asked.

"No, no," Mr. Haggard said, struggling to sit up as the attendant fastened straps across his torso. "I told you, I have no relatives. Only Rudy, my dog. This is Nick, the boy who takes care of Rudy for me. I was afraid you wouldn't come, boy, before they took me away."

Nick moved to the stretcher and stood close to the old man. "What happened?"

"My leg is worse. Hurt so bad I couldn't hardly stand it, all night. Must have been getting out of here in such a hurry last night. They may have to operate on it. Listen, boy, you stay over here and take care of Rudy, all right?"

"Sure, Mr. Haggard, I'll take care of Rudy," Nick assured him. He felt deeply sorry for the old man; pain was evident in his face.

"Be sure he gets his vitamins," Mr. Haggard said.

63

"Bottle just inside the cupboard. He won't eat his dog food unless you put the vitamins on it. And bring in my mail, will you? Don't get much that's important, except my pension check, but you bring it inside."

"Sure. I'll bring it to you in the hospital, if you want," Nick offered. It made him feel bad to see the old man suffering this way. "Don't worry about Rudy. I'll take good care of him."

The blanket was tucked around Mr. Haggard and the straps pulled tight enough to keep him in place when he was lifted into the ambulance. The men began to roll the gurney toward the door.

Rudy whimpered, knowing something was wrong, and Nick caught him by the collar and held him back. "Sit, boy," he said, and Rudy sat, though he continued to make sounds of distress, deep in his throat.

Nick got the dog's leash and slipped the choke chain over his head. He wasn't allowed to take the Airedale for a walk, though, not yet.

The stranger was still there in the hall, and he blocked the outside doorway. Nick had to stop, though Rudy strained at the leash in his eagerness to get out of doors.

"Excuse me," Nick said, but the man didn't move.

"My name's Howard. Paul Howard. I'm with the Fire Marshal's office," the man said, and Nick began to have an odd tingling sensation that was not at all pleasant. "I'd like to talk to you for a few minutes, young fellow."

Nick swallowed. "Yes, sir. Only Rudy hasn't been out yet this morning. Could I just take him back in the alley for a few minutes?"

"I'll walk there with you," Mr. Howard agreed. He nodded toward Mr. Hale and Mr. Griesner. "I'll be speaking with you gentlemen again."

It seemed almost a threat. And while Nick had no reason to feel guilty, no reason to worry about what the investigation would reveal, he couldn't help having a sense of apprehension.

"If it was kids, fooling around, I hope you put the fear of the law into them," Mr. Hale said sharply. "If the fire had had another ten minutes start before the alarm was turned in, I'd have lost the whole building."

"Not to mention the belongings of all of us that live here," Mr. Griesner added sourly. "And maybe even some of us, ourselves."

Mr. Howard allowed Nick and Rudy to go down the front steps, walking slightly behind them because that was the only safe place to be in relation to the Airedale. Otherwise, it was possible to be knocked down.

"Setting fires is a serious business," Mr. Howard said, as if Nick didn't know that. When Nick made no response, Mr. Howard added earnestly, as they reached the sidewalk, "It's better to admit to having made a mistake than to allow an expensive investigation to go on. It costs a lot of taxpayers' money to send men out to find out how a fire began, and it would be easier on every-body if the culprit simply told the truth. We don't put anybody in jail for accidentally starting a fire, you know."

Fear and anger welled up in Nick, and he didn't know which was the stronger emotion. He tried to speak, stumbling as Rudy jerked him off the curb, and his voice would not work at all.

"Do you like to watch fires?" Mr. Howard asked, pausing to allow Nick time to disentangle himself from Rudy's chain and get him back on the right course. "Lots of people do, they're fascinated by fire."

This time Nick managed to speak, though his voice squeaked. "I go watch a fire when there's one in the neighborhood, the same as anyone else," he said. "My dad always told me to keep well back out of the way of the fire fighters. And he taught me never to be careless with fire. I never have been, since I was a little kid."

He wondered what Mr. Howard would think if he knew about that one time, when Nick was six and Barney was eight, when they *had* played with matches, and set a grass fire that had nearly scared both of them to death. Luckily their father had been home and had come running with a hose and a shovel, and they hadn't needed the fire department to put it out; neither of the boys would ever forget the lecture they'd listened to once the danger was ended. Because Barney was older, and he was the one who'd actually gotten the matches out of the kitchen, he'd been most severely reprimanded. Yet Nick's ears felt blistered for weeks, and he'd never been tempted to experiment with fire after that. The idea of causing great damage and maybe even someone's death was enough to make him very careful from then on.

He gathered his courage now, looked directly at Mr. Howard, and said as forcefully as he could, "I didn't have anything to do with that fire last night, and neither did my friend Sam. It was just the way we told the fireman last night. Rudy heard something in the alley and barked, the way he does when he's surprised, and we looked that way and saw the little spark, and then all those boxes burst into flames. Sam ran to turn in the alarm and warn the people in the house, and I got the hose. That's all we had to do with it."

He was trembling a little, and he walked rapidly because Rudy was eager to go. Ordinarily Nick would have run with him, but he couldn't do that as long as Mr. Howard wanted to talk.

He hoped the man would believe him, but to his astonishment it was as if Nick had never said anything at all. As they turned into the familiar alley, still smelling of scorched wood and paper, the investigator said, "Sometimes a boy is so fascinated with fires that he sets them just to watch them burn, without considering the consequences in damage or lives. Sometimes he starts a fire to give himself a chance to be a hero. You know, to turn in the alarm and warn the people and help put the fire out."

Nick stopped in the middle of the alley so suddenly that Rudy skidded on the gravel and looked at him wonderingly. "I never did any of those things. I don't know if the fire was arson or an accident, but *I* didn't have anything to do with it. Sam and I were together, and both know the truth. Why don't you find out why the lights were out, the way Mr. Hale said? It sure made it dark enough back here in the alley so nobody could see what was going on, and it's peculiar the *two* street lights would go out at the same time. Besides the lights in the house and on the porch. And the can of gas in the closet under the stairs."

He hadn't meant to say that. He didn't know if any of the gas had been poured on the cardboard before the fire started or not; certainly he didn't remember smelling gasoline at the time, and the firemen were trained to notice things like that.

Mr. Howard's eyes narrowed and he stood with his hands in his pants pockets. "There's a can of gas in the closet in the Hillsdale Apartments?"

"Well, there was earlier in the week. I found it when I was looking for Eloise—a cat—and it was a red can and smelled of gasoline. Only it wasn't there when I looked again. I'd told Mr. Haggard about it, because Dad always said it wasn't safe to store things like that in a place where anything could catch fire. I suppose he told Mr. Griesner, and the can was moved to a better place."

Nick could tell by the expression on the man's face that he intended to pursue this matter further. He was sorry he'd mentioned it, because it might seem as if Nick were only trying to throw blame elsewhere to shift it away from himself.

"I'll ask the manager about it," Mr. Howard said. "Well, thank you for talking to me. I'll probably be around for a few days. I'll see you again, Nick."

Nick devoutly hoped that would not be the case, at least not if the authorities thought he was guilty of anything. When Mr. Howard turned to retrace his steps, Nick and Rudy sped down the alley, as if they could run away from whatever problems remained.

At the yard where Rudy had somehow been imprisoned the night before, a man came through the gate into the alley, and picked up a big metal garbage can. He put it down again and looked around, then glanced at Nick.

"You see an extra lid anywhere? Mine's missing."

"No, sir. I didn't notice one," Nick said, slowing to a walk.

"Darned garbage men, they're always losing the lids instead of putting them back where they belong," the man grumbled. He dropped a plastic sack into the can and went back inside the fence, latching the gate behind him.

Nick looked thoughtfully at the can beside the fence. If the lid had been on it last night, Rudy could easily have leaped onto the garbage can, then over the fence. And since there was nothing for the dog to climb on inside the fence, Rudy wouldn't have been able to get back out. He wished the Airedale could tell him what had happened. Had Rudy chased the person who started the fire? Or had he just run along because someone was running and Rudy loved to run?

He found the lid several houses away, as if it had rolled there, or been thrown, wedged between two more garbage cans that each had its proper cover. Nick picked it up and carried it along to see if it fit the open can.

It did, but not as well as it ought to. Because although it was a relatively new can—the bottom part had no dents in it at all—the lid was dented as if something heavy had damaged it. It would no longer stay tight on the can.

Not Rudy, Nick thought. Rudy wasn't heavy enough to have pushed it out of shape that way. He didn't think his own weight would bend it. But a heavier person might have done so. An adult.

Had someone run down the alley in the dark while Nick and Sam were acting upon the emergency of the fire? Someone who climbed on the garbage can and jumped over the fence, while Rudy chased after him?

It could have happened, Nick decided. Would the fire department investigator believe him if he saw the dented can lid and told him about Rudy being trapped inside the yard?

Or would the man think Nick had jumped on the lid until he dented it himself, and made up the entire story?

Certainly there was no proof of anything, only Nick's suspicions.

For a moment, before he moved on, Nick stared at the house inside the fence. If someone had fled the scene of the fire and vaulted the fence (possibly to escape Rudy)?, he must either have entered the house or gone through the yard and out into the street beyond. And he'd had very good luck to find the garbage can in the darkness.

Or, Nick suddenly realized, he could have scouted it out ahead of time, known where it was, even marked it in some way.

Rudy was running by this time, ears blowing back, and Nick ran with him, wondering if his old shoes would hold out for the rest of the summer with this kind of activity every day. Nick liked to run; it was one of the few athletic things he was good at--better than Barney, who could beat him at almost everything else—and usually he enjoyed it.

Today, though, it was hard to enjoy anything, though the sun was bright and the air was warm and he could run for an hour. Because Nick couldn't help thinking about the way Mr. Howard had acted as if he still suspected Nick and Sam of starting that fire.

Nick knew they hadn't, of course, and that started his thoughts on another train that wasn't any easier to deal with. Because if Nick and Sam hadn't started it, someone else had, and if it had been deliberate, that other person, or persons, hadn't cared if the house burned down and all the tenants and pets along with it.

And that, Nick thought, chilled, would have been not only arson but murder.

6

H E couldn't get the matter out of his mind. All the time he was feeding Fred and Maynard, and taking Maynard for *his* outing, Nick kept thinking about it.

He was still trying to figure out what had really happened when he came down the stairs and ran into Mrs. Sylvan.

"I'm glad I caught you," she said. "Even though it's the weekend, I'll be gone this afternoon and early this evening, and again tomorrow, so will you take care of Eloise just as you have been doing?"

Nick gave a sigh and agreed. He sure hoped Eloise would be better soon. Even the towel trick didn't help as much as it once had. Eloise was a pain. The only thing that kept him at it was the money.

He went back to Mr. Haggard's apartment and made sure Rudy had food and water. Rudy looked at the dish and then back at Nick, waiting.

"Well? What's the matter with you? Eat it," Nick said.

Still Rudy waited, giving his stubby tail a tentative twitch.

And then Nick remembered. Vitamins. Mr. Haggard had said Rudy wouldn't eat the food without the vitamins.

He found the bottle and measured out the amount it said for a dog Rudy's size. And sure enough, as soon as he'd done that, the big Airedale began to eat enthusiastically, crunching the hard bits as if they were bones being ground up by ogre teeth.

Nick watched him. Rudy could really run. If he'd chased anybody, could even a grown man have gotten completely away from him?

Nick didn't think so. Unless, of course, the man had a good head start. That might have happened.

If Rudy had closed those teeth on anybody, there surely would have been some noise Nick and Sam would have heard. Anybody would yell if a dog bit into his leg or his behind, wouldn't he?

He didn't know for sure that Rudy would have bitten anybody he chased. Rudy had been gentle as a lamb, as far as Nick had seen.

A stranger wouldn't know Rudy was running for fun, and might have been scared enough to do anything to get away. Still thinking it all over, Nick let himself out of Mr. Haggard's apartment and went to check the mailbox, in case the old man's pension check was there. He knew how elderly people had to be careful about those.

There were six boxes, and they had numbers on them made by the same crayon as had been used to mark the doors inside, but they were so smudged Nick couldn't really make them out. There was an official looking envelope protruding from one of the boxes, so Nick pulled it out and looked at it.

It was a check, all right; it showed through the window envelope. But it wasn't Mr. Haggard's pension, it was addressed to Clyde Foster, and it was from an insurance company. Nick dropped it back into the metal box and tried the next one.

There, that was Mr. Haggard's mail. No check, only two bills. Nick took them inside and put them on the table by the chair where the old man usually sat, anchoring them with a book so they wouldn't get knocked off.

"No, I'm not taking you out again," he told Rudy, who seemed as overjoyed at his appearance as he had been at the two earlier visits. "I'll be back later, though."

He opened the door into the hall and heard voices; it was the hippies, Clyde and Roy, coming in.

"Hey, they finally paid for that stuff we lost," Clyde said in a pleased tone. "Now maybe we can get us some furniture. Like a table and a couple of real chairs. And I need some more canvas to paint on."

"Wheels, man," Roy replied. "We need a set of wheels."

They closed the door behind them, not noticing Nick in the doorway of apartment one. They were talking about Roy's gig, which Nick decided meant a session of playing his guitar somewhere, and how it was about time the insurance company paid off.

Rudy nudged Nick's hand, and Nick scratched behind the animal's ears, eliciting a whimper.

"That feel good? Or are you already lonesome, because Mr. Haggard's gone to the hospital?" Nick looked at the Airedale in mild concern. He supposed pets were the same as people, in some ways; they didn't like being left alone, and there was no way to explain to them what had happened.

Overhead, the music came on as Clyde and Roy reached their apartment. Nick flinched. It was a good thing most of the residents in the house were either away or moderately deaf, he thought.

"Don't worry, I'll be back late this afternoon," he promised, and left Rudy whining behind the brown door. He wished he knew the truth about that fire in the alley; it would make a difference in what he decided to do, and right now he had the uneasy conviction that he ought to be here, taking care of the pets on the premises. During the day there was only Mr. Griesner —who didn't think much of pets—and sometimes Clyde and Roy at home, and at night Mrs. Sylvan. Mrs. Sylvan would get Eloise out if there was any need to do so; Nick wasn't so sure she'd consider saving Rudy and Maynard and Fred. And, of course, she didn't have keys to those apartments, anyway. He wasn't sure if Mr. Griesner did or not.

He ran on home, forgetting everything else as he sped along the quiet street. He loved to run; he forgot he was small for his age when he was running, and that Barney was a pest he had to share a room with, and all the other problems that cropped up when he allowed himself to think about them. Charles said if he kept in practice, they'd probably let him be on the track team by the time he got into high school. He thought it would feel good to run in competition with other kids from other schools, and maybe to win. Next year he planned to be one of the best runners in the seventh grade.

By the time he reached home, he imagined plunging

across the finish line and having the prize awarded to him. Only the illusion was somewhat spoiled when he felt a seam give on his shoes. Ruefully, Nick surveyed the damage. He'd break his neck if he didn't get that stitched back together before he tried running again. He wondered if he'd have to pay for the repair out of the 25 percent left from his earnings, or if Dad would consider shoe repair a family expense.

He found his father on the ladder around back, where he usually was when he wasn't at the hospital, carefully spreading yellow paint with a wide brush. Barney, eating a baloney sandwich, stood watching. Barney rolled his eyes at Nick.

"The rate he's going, he'll still be on the back part of the house at Christmas," he said.

"I hope not. How's Grandma?"

Mr. Reed heard his voice and turned to wave with the brush, sending a few drops of paint onto Nick's face. "Hi, Nick. Your mother went over to spend a few hours with her. It's amazing how fast people come around these days. With that steel pin in her hip, they're getting her up already. But she likes to have your Mom there."

"Will she be able to walk again all right?" Barney asked.

"They think so. It will take months of physical therapy, probably, before she gets anywhere near normal. Listen, boys, how about getting into some old clothes and giving me a hand? You could do that area beneath the windows, there."

"I didn't have much breakfast," Nick pointed out. "Go ahead, Barney, I'll join you in a few minutes."

Painting wasn't what he wanted to be doing, but Barney had a point. Their father was so meticulous and so bad at doing anything with his hands that he was very slow; if they didn't pitch in and help a little, there wouldn't be time to go to Disneyland or anywhere else before school started.

Actually, he didn't mind painting, once he got started. It was sort of fun to see how nice it looked after he'd run the brush along one of the boards, leaving a smooth clean surface. And it didn't take much concentration; there was plenty of time to think about other things.

The worst part of it was working next to Barney. Barney never shut up. And he didn't like the way Nick painted any more than he liked the way Nick kept his half of their room or anything else Nick did.

"You're dripping it on your shoes, idiot," Barney said.

"They're pretty well shot, anyway." Nick remembered then, and raised his voice. "Hey, Dad, should I get my running shoes repaired over at Hubble's? A seam broke."

"Fixing them's cheaper than new ones. Take a couple of dollars out of my wallet; it's on the dresser in my bedroom," Mr. Reed offered. He climbed down to move the ladder, and as long as he was within earshot, Barney kept still, but only until Mr. Reed disappeared around the corner.

"Be more careful around the windows, Nick. You're such a slob, you're getting it on the white part."

"That's going to be repainted, too. It's going to be white. So what hurt does it do if I get a little yellow there? I can go faster if I don't try to be so fussy."

"You're not too fussy, you don't have to worry about that," Barney said in obvious disgust. "Boy, Nick, you're a real pig."

For a moment Nick contemplated reaching out with a brushful of paint and slapping it right across his brother's mouth. The urge was so strong that it must have been written on his face, because Barney suddenly grinned.

"Go ahead, Nick, start something," he said.

The brush actually trembled in Nick's hand.

"Temper, temper, Nick," Barney said, waiting, ready to strike back immediately if his brother succumbed to his goading.

Nick wasn't sure what would have happened if they hadn't heard their mother coming right then. Probably he'd have poked the paint-laden brush in Barney's face, and Barney would have knocked him flat, and then Dad would have been mad at both of them.

As it was, Mrs. Reed came out onto the patio, looking very tired.

"How's Grandma?" the boys asked at the same time.

"Physically, she's pretty good. She's upset, though. Worried about the inconvenience she's causing the family, and about whether she'll be a burden if she can't walk without a walker. Has anyone had lunch yet?"

"No," Barney said. "You want me to help get something, Mom?"

How could he be so sweet and helpful sometimes, and so rotten the rest of the time? Nick wondered. None of that helpfulness came out in regard to Nick, that was certain.

They all gathered around the kitchen table, still wearing their painting clothes, to eat chicken salad sandwiches, milk, and cookies. Nick told them about Mr. Haggard going to the hospital, and the responsibility he felt about the animals.

"Mrs. Monihan wanted me to stay overnight at her place, to keep Fred and Maynard company. I haven't done it, and it's been kind of worrying me. And now Rudy's alone, too, with Mr. Haggard sick. I kind of wondered if maybe I *should* sleep over there, at least part of the time." Nick hesitated to see if they would immediately protest the idea, but only Barney responded.

"Great! Why don't you stay tonight, and I'll have Chuck stay overnight and sleep in your bed. I never can have a buddy stay overnight because there's no place for him to sleep."

"Well," Nick added, "there are plenty of other people in the house all the time. And Mrs. Monihan will pay me double if I stay overnight once in a while. I guess her pets are used to lots of company, and Rudy sure is. I could tell he missed Mr. Haggard already, because he whined when I left him."

His parents looked at each other. "I don't see any reason why you couldn't stay over there part of the time," Mr. Reed said. "Not move over, of course. There's no need for that. You can eat your meals at home, and check in with us regularly when you do stay. I assume all the apartments have their own phones, don't they?"

It was as easy as that. Nick wasn't sure if he'd really wanted them to agree or not, but it was settled now. He asked his mother to look in on Mr. Haggard the next time she visited his grandmother in the hospital, and after Mr. Reed had returned to his painting, Nick called Sam.

"How about staying with me? There's no Space Invaders game, but both apartments have TVs."

"OK. If Mom says it's all right, I'll meet you there after supper," Sam agreed. "We going to take anything along to eat?"

"There's still cookies at Mrs. Monihan's. I'll make some sandwiches, too, before I leave home," Nick promised. He felt better at the idea of having company his first night at the Hillsdale Apartments.

He did a little more painting with Barney that afternoon, got his shoe repaired, and then, after an early supper ran on over to Hillsdale Street. He didn't want Rudy to feel as if he'd been abandoned.

Once more there was a strange car in front of 1230. This was quite different from the Cadillac driven by Mr. Hale; instead it was a blue van painted to look as if it had flames coming out of the front end. At least, there were a few painted flames; Clyde was adding more, while Roy sat on the curb, wiggling his bare toes in time to the music he coaxed from his guitar.

Nick came to a halt. "Wow," he said.

Clyde looked up, grinning. "Like it?"

"It's great. Is it your car? Or are you doing it for someone else?"

"It's our car. We just bought it, a few hours ago, with part of the insurance check from when our stuff burned up. You know, we told you how we lost all our belongings in a fire over Jacobsmeyer's Drug Store. I'm painting it to use as an advertisement, to show people what I can do, right? So maybe someone will pay me to decorate their van; I did one once of a dragon rising out of the sea. It was really neat, but some drunk ran a stop sign and totaled the van. Sure ruined one of my best paintings."

"Did you get an insurance settlement on that one?" Nick asked. Something was pricking at the back of his mind.

"Oh, yeah, eventually." Clyde bent with the small brush and carefully outlined, freehand, another leaping flame in bright red. "That time I used the money to get some furniture, but then it burned up. Roy and I decided we'd be better off with a van than with furniture, anyway; and maybe with this I can stir up some business, earn a little money, you know?"

"I guess a lot of people would pay to have that kind of painting done," Nick said. He stood there for a few minutes, watching. He had no artistic ability whatever, and he admired it in someone else; Clyde was definitely talented. Nick imagined he could feel the heat from the greedy flames that licked the black stripe along the side of the van.

Walking Rudy a little later, though, he couldn't help thinking about a few things. He talked it over with Sam, after he and Rudy picked him up. Sam came out carrying a couple of cans of Pepsi and a bag of his mother's homemade doughnuts as his contribution toward the snacks.

Sam listened intently until Nick had finished.

"These guys told you that twice they've collected insurance money. Once when their van was wrecked and once when the stuff in their apartment burned up. You thinking maybe they had something to do with that fire here the other night? Like, they might want to collect again from the insurance company?"

Nick jerked on the leash to slow Rudy down. He couldn't carry on a conversation while running. Rudy looked at him, puzzled, but obediently slowed his pace.

"I don't know. I wouldn't want to accuse anybody of such a thing, but they're still investigating it as arson, and if it was, somebody had to set the fire. We know *we* didn't, whatever Mr. Conrad thinks. And Clyde and Roy have collected money before, because of a fire. It makes me wonder."

"You said you saw into their apartment, though, and it didn't have much in it. Sleeping bags on mattresses, and a stereo set. The insurance company wouldn't pay much for that kind of thing, would they? I mean, you'd have to have something worth insuring to make it worthwhile to destroy it and collect on it, wouldn't you?"

That was logical, Nick thought, relieved. "What little I saw was hardly worth insuring," he agreed.

"Of course, they weren't in the building when the fire started," Sam said, making Nick immediately uneasy again. "I wouldn't stay in the place if I intended to set it on fire. Not unless I was positive I could get out in time."

"I guess if anybody was setting a fire for profit, they'd have to have quite a bit at stake, more than Clyde and Roy, maybe. I can't imagine Mr. Haggard doing such a thing even if he could get around well enough, and Mrs. Monihan's gone, and Mrs. Sylvan . . ." He considered. He disliked her cat, and some of his feelings about Eloise sort of rubbed off onto the cat's owner. But he didn't seriously think such a dignified elderly lady would pile up boxes against the back of the house and set them afire. "Mr. Griesner, now, I don't like him much, but he was *in* the house. And what I saw, looking in through his door, didn't look very valuable to me. Not valuable enough to commit a felony to have somebody pay for it so you could do something with the money. The one who had the most to lose, if the house had burned to the ground, would be Mr. Hale, wouldn't it? I mean, he owns the house, and Mom says these old Victorian places are getting valuable now, like antiques."

"He wasn't in the alley," Sam said. "Not when the fire started. He was at a meeting of the City Council, making a speech. I know because my dad was listening to the news on the radio this morning and he heard about it. He mentioned it to my mom because he always gets mad about whatever the City Council decides to do. He always acts like all the money is coming out of his own pocket."

"Yeah, mine, too," Nick agreed. "Well, maybe it was just kids playing with matches, after all."

"Yeah," Sam said. And then, as they trotted along behind the big Airedale, he added, "Except it's funny about the lights, isn't it? The streetlights and the porch and hall lights. All going out at the same time."

"Just about the time you say something that makes me feel better, you follow it up with something that makes me feel worse," Nick told his friend. "Come on, let's run the rest of the way to the park."

By the time they came back, Clyde had finished painting his van, and they paused to look it over.

"He's pretty good," Sam conceded. "Do you think anybody would set a house on fire, though, in order to get a van so he could paint it like that?"

"Not really," Nick decided. "Come on, let's take Maynard on a run. We'll leave the stuff you brought in Mr. Haggard's refrigerator, OK?"

When they went into the house, Nick had the key out for Mr. Haggard's apartment. Only to his surprise, when Rudy moved ahead of him and nudged the door, it swung inward before Nick could get the key in the lock.

"Hey! I locked the door behind me, didn't I?"

Sam shrugged. "I don't know. I wasn't here. You must have forgotten to do it, Nick."

"Boy, I hope nobody got in and took anything." Nick slipped the choke chain over Rudy's head and glanced toward the mail he'd left on the table. "It doesn't look as if anybody's been here. I don't think Mr. Haggard has much to steal; his TV is OK."

"Ah, nobody could get in from the street anyway, could they? They'd have to have the key to the front door, and you didn't forget to lock that one."

"Yeah. I guess," Nick said. He was relieved that nothing had happened, yet disturbed that he could have left the door unlocked. The Reeds didn't lock their doors during the daytime, but it was different being responsible for someone else's home. He'd be careful never to forget the lock again, he thought.

They were on their way out with Maynard when they met Mr. Howard, the investigator from the fire department.

Nick's heart lurched in his chest. He would have gone on past with no more than a murmured greeting if the man hadn't blocked their way.

"Walking the dogs again?" Mr. Howard asked. It was an ordinary thing to say, but the way he said it wasn't ordinary. Nick didn't like the man looking at him in the way he did.

"Yes, sir," Nick said. "I do it every day. Several times a day."

Mr. Howard stood at the foot of the front steps looking at them, his hands in his trouser pockets. Because the boys were on the steps, Nick was on an eye level with the man.

"Have you thought any more about that gas can you said you saw in the closet under the stairs?" Mr. Howard asked.

The discomfort in his chest increased as Nick swallowed. "There wasn't anything in particular to think about it," he said. "First it was there, and then it wasn't. I suppose somebody took it away after I told Mr. Haggard about it being dangerous in there."

"And who do you think might have done that?" The question was put in a calm voice that didn't fool anybody. Beside him, Nick felt Sam stiffen.

"I don't have any idea, unless it was Mr. Griesner. He's the apartment manager; he'd take care of a thing like that."

"Only he didn't," Mr. Howard said. "He doesn't know anything about a gas can in the closet. Nobody told him about it, and he didn't move it."

"Neither did we," Sam said, indignation rising to match what Nick was feeling.

Mr. Howard had very sharp gray eyes. He fixed them on Sam. "Did you see the can, too?"

"No, but Nick said it was there, so it was. Nick's not a liar."

For just a moment, Nick thought the man was going to challenge that statement, and he almost forgot to breathe. Then Mr. Howard stepped aside and let them go, without making any further response at all.

"He doesn't believe us," Sam muttered under his breath as they strode away from the house.

"What does he think? That I made it up? If I'd had anything to do with a can of gas around the fire, does he

84

think I'd tell him about it? The heck with him. I don't care what he thinks. We didn't do anything wrong, and he can't prove we did."

Still, he couldn't help worrying about it as they walked on. Mr. Haggard hadn't been feeling well, and maybe he hadn't remembered to tell the manager about the gas can, and anybody in the house could have moved it. There hadn't been any smell of gasoline at the scene of the fire, so there was no reason to think it had had anything to do with that, was there?

So he didn't understand why it continued to bother Mr. Howard.

7

I T was a good thing Sam was with him that evening,
or Nick would never have gotten Eloise's medicine into
her. He had waited until after Maynard's walk, putting
it off as long as possible. Even with both of them chasing her into a corner, and Sam throwing the towel this
time to immobilize her, the cat managed not to swallow
about half of what they tried to put into her.

"What's wrong with her?" Sam asked. "She's too
strong to be very sick, seems to me." He sucked at a
scratch on his thumb.

"We better clean off your hand and put antiseptic
on it. I don't know what her problem is, and right now
I don't care. I wish I hadn't told Mrs. Sylvan that I'd
take care of her."

Eloise had retreated to the top of a china cabinet and
surveyed them with big, malevolent eyes, cleaning off
her white fur where the medicine had spilled.

"Why don't you tell Mrs. Sylvan you don't want to
give Eloise her medicine any more?" Sam asked. "She

probably wouldn't even want you to do it if she knew how we had to wrestle her around."

Nick shifted his weight from one foot to the other, staring at the cat. "I don't know. For one thing, I don't know who else she'd get to do it. I mean, can you imagine Mr. Griesner or Clyde and Roy coming in to give medicine to a stuck-up cat? And I agreed to do it, so I'm sort of obligated. Dad says if you agree to do something, you should follow through even if it turns out it's not as good a deal as you expected it to be. It's kind of a challenge, I guess."

Sam pushed back the lock of red hair that had fallen forward. "I suppose I wouldn't like it, either, if somebody held me down and put nasty tasting stuff into me. Oh, well, come on. Let's get out of here and feed Maynard and Fred. I like them a lot better."

It was easy to like Maynard and Fred. They were both friendly, and Maynard, especially, was cute. He knew how to lie down on command, to sit, to beg, to shake hands, and to fetch things. Fred didn't do any tricks, but the big gray striped cat would rub against them and his rumbling purr was clear evidence that he liked them, too.

When all their chores were over, they had to decide where to spend the night. "Maybe you should stay one night with Rudy, and the next one with Maynard and Fred," Sam suggested. "That would be fair to everybody."

"I'm getting the extra pay to stay with Maynard and Fred," Nick pointed out. "Only of course before Rudy wasn't alone, and in some ways he's a bigger baby than Maynard. At least Maynard has Fred to keep him company. And the two of them don't really seem to mind being alone the way Rudy does."

"I wonder if we could take them all into the same apartment? Would that work? Then everybody would keep everybody else company."

It sounded like a good idea, except for one thing. "Rudy chases cats," Nick remembered. "I don't think Fred would put up with much of that."

They decided to walk the dogs again, at the same time, with Nick handling the Airedale and Sam holding the leash for the little mop dog. Outside of the fact that Rudy didn't seem to notice when he stepped on Maynard in the excitement of getting started on an extra walk, the dogs got along together all right.

When they came back, it was nearly dark. The newly painted van belonging to Clyde and Roy was gone; in its place was a beat up old pickup. A man in coveralls was getting a tool box out of the back of it, looking up to the sign identifying the building; a companion sat behind the wheel.

"You kids live here?" the man asked as they passed him and turned in.

"No. I mean, we're staying here for now, taking care of some dogs and cats," Nick said.

The man was young, with a sandy mustache and rather longish hair under his cap that matched the coveralls. A name, *Al*, was embroidered over his breast pocket.

The driver got out and came around the front of the truck. He was very skinny and dark haired, and over his coverall pocket was the name *Greg*.

"This the right place?" he asked.

"Hillsdale Apartments, right?" Al said, and Nick

nodded. "OK. The manager is supposed to live in the back. Do we ring the front doorbell, or go around the side?"

"I think he'll come if you ring the bell," Nick said.

"You got a key to the front door?" Al looked at the ring of keys Nick had taken out of his pocket. "No need to bother the manager if you kids can let us in."

Nick stared at him. "I don't have any right to let anybody in except me, to take care of the dogs."

"Hey, we're not here to rip anybody off," Al said, and laughed. He had crooked teeth. "The owner sent us, to do some repairs."

"Funny time to start a job like that, this late on Saturday," Sam said.

"Well, we have to work at night and on weekends because we're doing this on the side. We work regular jobs in the daytime. Besides we're just here to look things over," Al told them. "It don't make no difference to me if you don't want to let us in. Ring the bell, Greg, and get the manager. We'd ought to tell him we're here, anyway."

Nick felt a little bit silly, letting himself and Sam and the dogs inside and leaving the newcomers to stand on the porch waiting for Mr. Griesner to answer the bell. But it wasn't his house, and he didn't intend to be responsible for anyone getting into it. He inserted the key into Mr. Haggard's door, nearly tripping up when the dogs wound both leashes around his legs so that Sam had to disentangle them.

Mr. Griesner, wearing his usual soiled trousers and a plaid flannel shirt, came toward them in the dimly lighted hallway.

"What's going on? You kids monkeying with the bell?"

"No, sir," Nick said. He got the door open, and Rudy pushed past him into the apartment. Sam dragged Maynard inside, too. Behind them, they overheard the manager and the repairmen.

"Whatta you want?"

"Mr. Hale sent us. Do some repairs, you know?"

"He didn't say anything to me about sending anybody over. What do you mean, comin' at a time like this."

"You reported stuff needing repairs, didn't you? We came to look it over. Call him up and ask him. We can wait. He's paying us by the hour, so it don't matter to us how long it takes," Al said.

Nick closed the door on the conversation. Maynard was sniffing the unfamiliar quarters; Rudy waited expectantly with his tongue lolling out for his treat.

"I don't know about Fred, but these two are OK together," Sam said. "Where's this dog biscuit Rudy's supposed to get? I suppose I'd better give Maynard one, too, OK?"

"In the cupboard under the sink," Nick said. "A red and yellow box."

He was busy drawing the shade over the big colored glass window onto the street; he felt as if they were on exhibition otherwise, even if the window was high off the street. He turned around when he heard Sam's surprised grunt.

"Hey, Nick! Look what's under here. The gas can you were talking about." Sam lifted it and shook it. "It's just about full, too. The old man must have taken it out of the closet and brought it over here."

Nick frowned. "Why would he do that? I mean, it would be Mr. Griesner's job to get rid of it, and under Mr. Haggard's sink isn't a very good place to store it."

"No better than the closet," Sam agreed. "Especially with the junk he's got under here."

Nick stared into the compartment. Had it all been there before: the stack of rags and a paper bag full of burnable refuse? He didn't remember noticing it the times he'd gotten out the "cookies."

"I don't think we'd better leave it there. When I told him about it, Mr. Haggard didn't act like it was his can."

"What'll we do with it?" Sam set the red can on the counter and brought out the bone shaped dog biscuits, making both dogs sit up for their treats. "Take it back to Mr. Griesner?"

"Grouchy as he is, he probably wouldn't appreciate having his TV watching interrupted again. I ought to call up that Mr. Howard and show him the can. At least then he wouldn't think I made it all up."

"And it's full, so nobody used it to start any fire," Sam said. "You know how to reach Mr. Howard?"

"No," Nick admitted. "I don't even remember his first name, so I probably couldn't find him in the book. Well, give me the can. I'm going to put it outside, around the corner of the house, behind those bushes. Nobody'll steal it from there, if it's out of sight, and it's not likely to do any damage from there before I can show it to Mr. Howard."

"Maybe it's got fingerprints on it," Sam suggested. "Maybe they can tell who handled it."

"Sure," Nick said. "It's got yours and mine. What's that going to prove?"

He put the can safely outside and returned to find Al and Greg in the front hallway, with Greg writing down things on a paper and talking as he wrote. "Fix that broken board on the back step. Shore up the railing to the outside stairs where it goes across the roof. Replace the linoleum here by the stairs. Check to see how the wiring looks for these front lights. What else did you want to check, Al?"

"He said something about water stains on the wallpaper upstairs. Maybe a leak in the roof."

"Hale's going to blow his stack if he needs a whole new roof," Greg observed, with the objective air of one who isn't going to have to pay the bills. "How do we get in the attic to see where it's coming through?"

Nick was in the act of closing Mr. Haggard's door when Al's eyes met his. "You know, kid? Is there a stairway to the attic?"

Nick shook his head. "I don't know. I told you, I don't live here."

"You staying here for now, though?" Al laughed, looking around the gloomy entryway. "Spooky old place, isn't it?"

"He's right about that," Sam observed when Nick had closed the door. "It's like one of those places in the movies, where a ghost comes floating down the stairs and everybody's found murdered in their beds in the morning."

"Just because it's old doesn't mean it's haunted," Nick told him. "What are we going to watch on TV?" Sam had turned the set on.

"Reruns, I guess. There doesn't seem to be anything else." Sam settled into a corner of the shabby couch and allowed Maynard to crawl into his lap. "Good thing

Rudy's willing to stay on the floor. If he got into your lap, he'd squash you flat."

As it was, the Airedale chose to rest his head against Nick's foot, as if he drew comfort from the contact with a human being. He misses the old man, Nick thought, and reached out a hand to stroke the big head.

From time to time they heard hammering as Greg and Al seemed to be testing various parts of the building. Finally, with much banging and bumping around, the repairmen let themselves out and drove away in the pickup.

"I guess it's time we went to bed, huh?" Sam asked, yawning. "We've eaten everything we brought with us."

"OK. I'm tired, too. I suppose I better go up and check on Fred first. Do you think I should bring him down here, too? I'd hate to have Rudy go for him and wreck something."

"I'll put the choke chain on Rudy and hold him while you hold Fred," Sam proposed. "If it looks like it'll get wild, you can always put Fred back in his own apartment."

Nick felt strange climbing the stairs in the quiet house. It was different at night. Spooky, just as Al had said. Nick knew that Mr. Griesner was home, downstairs in the back of the house. And probably Mrs. Sylvan was home, too, though he hadn't heard her come in.

Up here on the second floor there was no one but himself. No music throbbed behind the door of Clyde and Roy's apartment. The stairs creaked even under Nick's meager weight, and though the bulb was on in the upper hallway, it didn't produce much light.

Nick let himself into Mrs. Monihan's apartment, and

was halfway across the living room toward Fred when an odor reached him. For a few seconds he didn't identify it, and then he did.

Hot. Something was hot, burning.

Panic gushed through him; for a moment he almost turned and ran, but reason took over almost immediately. It wasn't a fire, not yet, he thought. Something was simply overheated.

He went into the kitchen and reached for the light switch, staring at the electric stove. One of the burners glowed crimson, and smoldering at the edge of the red circle was a cereal box that had fallen over onto the element.

Nick reached for a spatula from the set of utensils on the wall and pushed the blackening carton into the sink. When he ran water on it, charred bits of cardboard flaked off and gave off an odor much like the one he'd smelled in the alley.

Nick turned off the burner and waited until the heat and color faded from it, inhaling deeply so that his breathing slowed to normal.

Who had turned the burner on? It couldn't possibly have been on ever since Mrs. Monihan left to visit her sister. Nick knew he would have noticed it.

He'd been in the kitchen several times a day, to put out fresh water and food for Maynard and Fred. Fred followed him now, leaping onto a chair, switching his long, thick tail.

Could Fred have been on the counter and knocked over the cereal box so that it fell across the burner? Yes, Nick decided, that could have happened. He wiggled the knob experimentally. Could Fred have accidentally turned it on if he'd brushed against it? Even now the big cat sprang onto the window sill looking out over the back stairs; obviously he wouldn't have any problem leaping onto the counter and the stove.

It didn't seem likely that a cat brushing against the knob could have turned it, but how else could it have gotten on?

Nick made sure the cereal box was soaked and no longer dangerous, then scooped up Fred and locked the door behind them to return downstairs.

"I don't think it's safe to leave you alone in there," he muttered, while Fred purred his pleasure at the attention.

Fred was not quite so pleased when he was carried into Mr. Haggard's living room. He stopped purring and glared at Rudy, who leaped up to meet him, restrained by the choke chain.

"I thought you were never coming back," Sam complained. "Once I got the chain on him, Rudy figured we were going for another walk, and it was all I could do to keep him still."

Nick related what had happened. "Do you think a cat could turn on a burner on the stove?"

"I don't know. Maybe. Fred's a strong cat. Anyway, you caught it in time. Put him down, Nick, see what happens."

What happened left them both shaken. For though they had thought themselves prepared to handle the situation if Rudy and Fred took a dislike to each other, they had underestimated both Rudy's strength and the determination of both animals.

Nick squatted down with Fred in his arms, intending

to protect the cat while allowing Rudy to get acquainted with him, perhaps touching noses, while Sam held the leash.

Rudy lunged forward to touch noses, all right, and Fred freaked out. Fred knew that Maynard was a friend, but all other dogs were enemies. He swiped his claws across the end of Rudy's nose; the Airedale yelped and pounced. Fred escaped from Nick's arms and fairly flew to the back of the nearest chair and then onto a bookcase, and from there atop a tall cabinet.

In the confusion, the leash was ripped out of Sam's hands and Nick was knocked flat on his back, with Rudy running right over him in a frantic attempt to capture the cat.

Standing on his hind legs, barking, Rudy was almost able to reach poor Fred, who arched his back, spat, and backed as far away as he could get.

Nick scrambled to his feet. "Down, Rudy! Sit! Sit, boy!"

Rudy was too excited to hear him. He leaped upward, sending Fred into a snarling fury as he first pressed against the wall and then sailed over the dog's head in a performance worthy of a circus aerialist toward the nearest tall object.

Unfortunately, that object was Sam's head. Sam, who had grabbed for the leash and was trying to pull Rudy away, instinctively staggered backward when the cat tried to secure his position with his claws, and boy and cat went down in a sprawl that carried Mr. Haggard's floor lamp with them.

There was a popping sound, and that light went out. Luckily they'd left the light on in the kitchen, so they weren't in darkness, but they were in chaos.

Nick crawled toward Rudy, who now had Fred cornered atop the TV; Nick had a few horrified moments hoping Rudy wouldn't knock it over, too, and then he got his arms around the Airedale's neck and pulled him away, speaking as sharply as he could considering he'd had the wind knocked out of him.

"Stop it, Rudy! Sit! SIT, darn it!"

Sam, too, had gotten to his knees. He surveyed the damage, looking dazed, until Nick said, "Catch Fred, Sam, and get him out of here. We'll have to put him back upstairs. The key's in my pocket, but I can't get it until you get Fred out of sight."

Maynard, confused and upset by all the commotion, had retreated to a corner of the couch; now he began to bark furiously.

When it was all over, and Fred and Maynard had been delivered back to their own apartment—they'd decided that since Fred was obviously upset, he'd be better off in Maynard's company—the boys ruefully examined Mr. Haggard's belongings. The lamp was broken, but Sam was sure his father could fix it for them. There was a rip in one of the sofa pillows; it was on a seam, so Nick figured he could repair that himself if his mother had any thread the right color. Various books and papers had been knocked onto the floor, though none of them seemed a serious casualty.

Sam bent his head and pulled his hair to each side so that Nick could examine his scalp. "It felt like I was gouged with red hot pinchers. Am I bleeding?"

"Only a little bit," Nick reported. "Maybe we better see if we need shots or something, with all this scratching. I've got a few marks, too." The places where Rudy's claws had sunk into his arm were beginning to hurt. "Only if I explain to my mom how it all happened, she'll probably make me quit this job. As it is, I'm at least out the price of a new lightbulb, even if your dad can fix the lamp. What will we tell him about it?"

"That it got knocked over. I don't have to tell him everything. Boy, we're lucky, the way those animals were leaping around here, that nothing more expensive was broken."

It was some time before they were able to settle down and go to sleep. Mr. Haggard's bed was different from the ones they were used to, and the old house creaked and groaned as if it were a living thing.

"My grandma's house is like this," Sam said, curled under the quilts. "Only in her house it didn't seem so scary."

"It's the wood contracting as it cools off," Nick offered, not admitting that he, too, found it sort of spooky.

He didn't know how late it was when he was roused by some sound outside Mr. Haggard's apartment.

Nick raised himself groggily onto an elbow, for a moment uncertain as to where he was. Then he heard Sam breathing beside him, and on the floor at the side of the bed, Rudy whuffed a warning.

Nick was suddenly cold, though he was still covered with the quilts to the middle of his chest. "What's the matter, boy?" he whispered.

As if in reply, Rudy whuffed again, and stood up. Nick stretched out a hand and felt the wiry hair bristling on the big dog's neck as a deep rumble issued from his chest.

"What's the matter?" Sam asked sleepily, and then,

when he came more fully awake, his voice changed to a sharper tone. "What's Rudy growling at?"

"I think there's someone in the hall," Nick said.

His heart was beating so hard it was a wonder he could hear anything else, but he did.

Footsteps sounded faintly through the wall, until Rudy actually barked, a great, deep bark such as only a very large dog can produce.

The footsteps ceased, and the boys waited, holding their breaths, Nick's hand on Rudy's head to quiet him, for whatever was going to happen next.

8

"MAYBE it's just those guys upstairs, coming home late," Sam whispered.

"Rudy's used to them by now. He doesn't bark at them. Besides, whoever it is didn't go up the stairs; they're right on the other side of this wall, in the hall-way."

They didn't hear any more, however. Whoever had made the sounds realized he'd wakened the dog and was being more careful. After a time Nick felt the tension go out of him, at least most of it did.

"What time is it, anyway?" Sam asked, keeping his voice very low.

"Turn on the light, and we'll see."

It was a quarter past three on Sam's watch. Somehow neither of them wanted to turn the light off and go back to sleep. Nick got up to get a drink, and Sam trailed along into Mr. Haggard's tiny kitchen, where they decided to make cocoa.

"I'd make a sandwich if I saw anything to make it

out of," Nick observed, looking in the cupboard. "There's a can of chili. How about some chili?"

So they heated that, and gave Rudy an extra couple of dog biscuits, huddling on the couch with Mr. Haggard's lap robe over their bare legs because it was cold in the room.

Rudy lay at their feet. Once he lifted his head to listen, cocking his head to one side. Immediately Nick's stomach muscles tightened again and he put aside his empty bowl, straining to listen, too.

Far away, through several doors and up the stairs, they heard the yapping of a small dog.

"Maynard," Sam said unnecessarily. "Nick, there's gotta be someone prowling around, or the dogs wouldn't keep acting funny, would they? If they act like this every time somebody who lives in the house moves around, nobody'd ever get any sleep in this place."

"I don't suppose people walk around in the middle of the night very often. The dogs might just be barking about that, even if it's somebody they know," Nick said, his voice sounding hollow. "Maybe we should go check on Maynard. Maybe it isn't a person, at all, but Fred's turned on the stove again or something. Maynard might bark if there was smoke. Dogs do that all the time."

For a moment neither of them moved. Nick almost wished he hadn't mentioned checking; he had no desire to unlock the door of Mr. Haggard's apartment and go out into the hallway.

Upstairs, Maynard barked again. Rudy rose from his place on the rag rug and went to the door, putting his nose to the crack. By now they ought to have been getting used to that *whuffing* noise he made, not quite a bark but more than a whimper.

Nick moistened his lips. "I guess we really better see what's the matter with Maynard," he said, hoping Sam would contradict him, wishing he'd stayed at home tonight instead of letting one of Barney's friends sleep in his bed.

"Yeah. Let's get dressed and go see," Sam agreed.

They debated whether to take Rudy with them or leave him locked in the apartment. "Let's take him," Nick decided.

The streetlights had been repaired, but when Nick opened the door the windows in the front doors glowed with muted reds, golds, greens and blues that did nothing to diminish the blackness. Mr. Griesner turned off the inside lights when he went to bed, and Nick felt oddly nervous crossing to flip the switch beside the front door, even with Sam right behind him.

The hallway was quite ordinary with the light on. Maynard had stopped barking now, but Rudy pushed against Nick's leg, quivering with eagerness to do something.

"The outside door's locked," Nick observed, trying it. "There couldn't be anybody inside that didn't have a key. I guess we'd better check on Maynard and Fred, anyway."

They delayed long enough to put Rudy on his leash, then mounted the creaking stairs, the dog eagerly leading the way.

"I'd have nightmares, living in this house," Sam muttered as one step gave a particularly loud protest under his weight. "I hope that's all that's the matter with Maynard, that he's having a bad dream."

Nick realized, when they reached the upper hall, that he was trying to smell smoke, and that there wasn't any. There was no sound behind the door of apartment three; either Clyde and Roy were asleep and hadn't heard anything, or they hadn't come in yet.

"Maybe you better keep Rudy out here," Nick suggested, fitting the key into the door across the hall. "So Fred doesn't break anything more, trying to get away from him."

Maynard met him with ecstatic yapping, throwing his small body against Nick's legs. Fred, curled in a big chair, opened one eye and then closed it again when Nick turned on the lamp.

There was nothing wrong in the place that Nick could see. The stove was still off, the way it was supposed to be. He pushed aside the curtains and stared out at the house next door. It stood dark and silent, its occupants sleeping. "Nothing going on over there to make him bark," Nick said, and dropped the curtains back into place.

He knew the back door that opened onto the outdoor stairs was locked, but he tried it anyway. There was a bolt that hadn't been secured, and he slid that into place just to make certain there was no access from the alley.

"Come on, let's go back to bed," Sam called, and Nick rejoined him.

"OK. I can't find anything to get Maynard excited. Maybe they both heard something we didn't hear, outside."

Neither of them mentioned the footsteps they'd heard earlier in the lower hallway. That was what had started the whole thing, waking them up and disturbing Rudy.

Nick checked the doors again before they went to bed. He didn't feel much like sleeping; he was more than ever aware of every sound in the big old house. He didn't hear any more footsteps, and finally Sam began to breathe regularly in sleep beside him.

Somewhere in the distance a siren rose and fell. He didn't know if it was a fire truck or an ambulance or a police car, but it sent chills through him so that he moved closer to Sam's warmth. Rudy slept on, undisturbed. Apparently Rudy was used to sirens, or didn't pay any attention to sounds that far away.

What was he going to do tomorrow night, Nick wondered, if Sam couldn't stay with him again?

He didn't have nerve enough to bring the subject up right away. They walked the dogs, put out fresh food and water, and then both headed for their own homes for breakfast, after deciding that another can of chili wasn't exactly what they wanted so early in the morning.

In the daylight they laughed about being scared during the night. Nothing had happened, had it? They'd heard some unexplained sounds, and that was all. In the bright sunshine the old house was just an old house, nothing sinister about it.

Sam didn't say anything about meeting Nick again that day. They walked together part way, and Nick almost called after him when Sam left to go toward his own home, but something kept him from it. Nick hated to admit he was a coward, even to his best friend.

Well, he thought, trudging up his own walk, night was a long way off, and he had plenty of time to talk to Sam again. Besides, there was no law that said he *had* to stay at 1230 Hillsdale tonight. He didn't have to stay every night. But if he didn't stay tonight, he ought to go tomorrow. Maybe today he'd just walk Maynard an extra time, during the afternoon, so that the pets wouldn't be alone for so long each day. After finding that stove burner on, he felt as if he ought to check fairly frequently, anyway, just in case Fred accidentally turned it on again.

The Reed household was the same as usual. Mrs. Reed was making waffles for breakfast, with delicious little sausages. It wasn't the right time to discuss last night with anybody, Nick decided, not with everyone making plans and hurrying to get ready for church. Molly was wiping up Winnie's spilled orange juice, the phone was ringing with a call for Charles asking him to come in early to work an extra shift, and Mr. Reed trying to talk all of the boys into helping with the painting.

"Charles can't today, if he's going to work two shifts. How about you, Barney? Surely you don't have any lawns to cut on Sunday."

Barney had just taken an enormous bite of syrup-soaked waffle and had to chew before he could reply, but his face was eloquent.

"Hey, Dad, it's not written on my schedule, but I have plans for this afternoon. Important plans!"

"Oh? Something you can't change? I really need help with the painting, kids; it's a big job, painting the whole house. Your mother intended to help with it on weekends, but with Grandma in the hospital she has to spend most of her free time over there, which leaves it up to me and you. All of you."

"Well, this is important to me," Barney said. "I met this . . . this kid I'm going to play tennis with. I promised. A new kid in town, who doesn't know anybody else in town to play with. And I don't know how to get in touch to cancel or anything, even if I wanted to. I haven't had much time to do anything for fun so far this summer."

It was Charles who was perceptive enough to guess the truth. "This kid a girl, Barney?"

To Nick's mingled delight and envy, Barney blushed. He didn't remember ever seeing his brother blush before.

"Well, so she's a girl, what difference does that make? I said I'd meet her, and since I can't tell her . . . I have to meet her, don't I?"

"Maybe you could meet her and tell her you have to paint the house," Winnie suggested, holding out her glass for more juice. "Maybe she'd like to come and help you paint."

Barney rolled his eyes. "Oh, sure! Some date that would be! Listen, Dad, I don't have a job tomorrow afternoon, and I'll help you from noon on, OK? Only I really want to play tennis today."

Nick wondered if he'd ever get to play tennis with a girl. Or do anything interesting with a girl, since so many of them were taller than he was, and they all seemed to prefer the taller boys. He didn't really see why it mattered so much, which person was taller, but it seemed to be important to most people.

Barney pushed back his chair, looked at the clock, and speared one more sausage. "Oh, I invited Chuck to stay over again tonight, Nick."

Nick stopped chewing. "Hey, I didn't give up my half of the room permanently, you know."

"Well, he's not coming tonight anyway. Has to go

someplace with his folks. But he is coming tomorrow. We want to finish our Monopoly game, OK?" Barney paused then, surveying Nick with slightly narrowed eyes. "How was it, sleeping in that old mausoleum? Kind of spooky?"

Mausoleum, if Nick remembered correctly, meant a place where they buried the dead, or was it stored them in crypts? He thought he detected a certain malicious amusement in Barney's gaze, and he made his reply casual, though he didn't feel that way about it. "It's just an old house, is all."

"No spooks? No ghosts?" Barney grinned. "Of course you had Sam there with you, didn't you? It would take a brave ghost to take old Sam on, I guess. Big as he is. So you weren't scared, huh?"

After that, how could Nick admit that he had been, for a time, scared spitless? And it looked as if he had to spend tomorrow night at 1230 Hillsdale, whether he wanted to or not.

He thought about it through the day as he went to church, helped paint the house for a while, and walked Maynard and Rudy both in midafternoon and evening, not to mention spending forty-five frustrating minutes medicating Eloise.

It was stupid, Nick thought bitterly. Why hadn't he admitted that he had been scared last night? If there was really something dangerous in the house wouldn't it be smarter to admit it, and stay away from it, than to pretend there was nothing the matter and maybe get hurt? Especially if it only meant that he was saving face in front of Barney. What did he care what Barney thought?

The trouble was, though, that he *did* care what

Barney thought. Or at least he cared about what Barney said. Barney had a way of not letting him forget it if he ever made a mistake. It never seemed to occur to him that Nick had feelings, too, and that it hurt to be taunted long after the episode should have been forgotten. Well, he had until tomorrow night to work something out.

Mr. Haggard's pension check came the next morning, and Nick took it inside. After the skirmish between Fred and Rudy on Saturday, he had decided to find a safer place to put the mail, in the drawer of a bureau. That afternoon, after a morning of painting and a check on all the animals, he decided to go over to the hospital and tell Mr. Haggard that the check was safe, and that Rudy was all right, too. He didn't let himself think it was a way of keeping busy, of not thinking about the night to come. He hadn't heard a word from Sam. And somehow he couldn't bring himself to call. Yet, with or without Sam, he, Nick, was committed to spending the night at 1230 Hillsdale.

Mr. Haggard looked even older than before, propped against pillows with his hair standing in white wisps. He grinned when he saw Nick, though, and lifted a hand in greeting.

"Well, fancy that, I've got a visitor! How are you, Nick?"

Nick relayed all his messages, glad he had come since the old man seemed so pleased to see him. Before he lost his courage, he blurted out the details of the mishap with the lamp and the pillow, though he left out the reason for Rudy's wild reaction. Maybe Mr. Haggard wouldn't like it that he'd brought someone else's animals into his apartment.

108

"My friend says his dad can fix the lamp. And I sewed up the rip in the pillow," Nick said.

Mr. Haggard didn't seem too upset. What mattered to him was that Rudy was OK. They talked on a bit and then just before he was ready to leave, Nick remembered the gas can.

Mr. Haggard looked bewildered. "Gas can? Well, I do remember you told me about it, and I meant to mention it to Mr. Griesner so he could move it, but my leg was hurting so bad—and those pain pills don't exactly make a fellow any smarter—I don't think I did it. And *I* sure didn't move it out of the closet into the cupboard under my sink. No, sir, I don't store any gasoline in the house. I knew a fellow, once, had some in his garage, and it exploded. He had third degree burns."

Nick listened to the details, wondering if Mr. Haggard could possibly have moved the can and forgotten it. The old man's mind seemed perfectly clear now.

If Mr. Haggard hadn't put the can under his sink, who had?

Walking down the broad tiled corridor toward his grandmother's room, Nick remembered uneasily that Mr. Haggard's apartment had been unlocked that one time he'd returned from a walk, even though he thought he'd locked it when he left. Someone else *could* have moved the gas can inside then, though he didn't see why they would have.

Talking to his grandmother took his mind off the situation at 1230 Hillsdale for a while. She, too, seemed smaller and older than he remembered. It was almost as if the hospital beds had the power to shrink people.

She was cheerful, though, and glad to see him. "I saw

the x-ray of the pin they put in my hip," she told him, and gestured with her hands about a foot and a half apart. "It's this long, and bent on the top where it goes through the hip joint, and it has what look like bolts through it, crossways, to hold it in place."

Nick swallowed. "Does it hurt a lot?"

"Well, it does when they make me move around. Would you believe the physical therapy department is making me *walk* already? I wasn't sure I'd ever walk again after an injury like that, but they get somebody on each side of me to get me up, and then I have a walker to hang onto, so I won't fall down. And it hurts, all right, though they said the more I walk, the less I'll feel it. Tomorrow I'm going to try crutches, and learn to go up and down steps. Imagine, so soon!"

"I think that's great, that you aren't going to be crippled or anything," Nick said.

His grandma reached out and squeezed his hand. "I think it's great, too, even if it does hurt right now. Thank you for coming to see me, Nick."

It almost made *him* hurt, to think about having a huge steel pin bolted through bone, even somebody else's bone.

Visiting his grandmother and Mr. Haggard in the hospital gave him something to think about as he walked on home. Getting old wouldn't be so bad if you didn't get sick or hurt, he thought. He wondered if Grandma would be able to play ball with them any more, or work in her garden the way she liked to do. He sure hoped so. If she couldn't, it would be the same as if *he* were no longer able to run.

The aroma of chicken met him at the front door.

Everybody else was at the table, and they looked up when Nick walked in.

"You're late," Winnie piped. "We're having fried chicken, Nick. I got a leg."

"Nick gets the tail," Barney offered. "He's the last one here, he gets the back end of the chicken."

Nick ignored him as he slid into his place and spoke to his parents. "I went over to the hospital to see Grandma and Mr. Haggard." In a sudden rush of words that showed the subject was still there, pushed to the back of his mind, he said, "Dad, could I talk to you for a few minutes tonight? After supper?"

"My bowling night, Nick, remember? Though I'm so stiff from standing on that ladder all day I'll be lucky to keep the ball out of the gutter. Here, how about a thigh? Or would you rather have half a breast?"

Nick chose the chicken thigh, accepted a mound of mashed potatoes, poured gravy over it, and allowed his mother to serve him the peas. He watched the butter melt on a hot biscuit and felt tension building up inside him. He hadn't consciously made the decision before, but he knew he'd been working up to it all day, to talk to his father about the things that had been happening at 1230 Hillsdale Street. He didn't know if he was imagining things or not, but if it was really dangerous to stay there, it was stupid to do it. His father wouldn't be like Barney, making fun of him for being afraid. Nick knew he could talk to his father.

Only he'd forgotten it was bowling night. And by the time his father came home, he'd already have to be going to bed over at the Hillsdale Apartments.

As usual, almost everybody had to go somewhere.

Molly was to clean up the kitchen before she went out to a movie with a girl friend. Mrs. Reed was, of course, going back to the hospital. Charles was already at work. Barney was baby-sitting Winnie and having his friend Chuck over and they were going to finish their Monopoly game and work on Barney's bike.

Nick knew without asking that his mother didn't have time to listen to him, either. If she'd had time, she would have helped with the kitchen cleanup, and he knew if she was late for visiting hours she sometimes had to park blocks from the hospital. She'd worked all day, and she was too tired to walk very far.

So there he was, with it time to head for Hillsdale Street and no chance to talk to anybody about any of what he was thinking. He called Sam's house, hoping Sam was going to be able to stay with him again tonight. By tomorrow, Nick promised himself, he'd get his father alone and have a serious conversation with him.

Only Sam wasn't home.

"I'm sorry, Nick. My husband decided to take a couple of days' vacation, and he and Sam went off to Willow Creek yesterday, on the spur of the moment," Mrs. Jankowski told him. "They intended to be back tonight, but they just called to say they're going to stay on and won't be in until tomorrow afternoon."

Tomorrow afternoon. Nick felt as if he'd been hit in the stomach as he replaced the phone. What about tonight?

9

H E supposed he could get out a sleeping bag and put it on the floor in Winnie's room. Winnie wouldn't care. But then there would be Barney and his big mouth. It had happened so often that Nick could almost see the scene unrolling like a movie in his mind. Barney's nasty smile, his taunting voice. "What's the matter, Nicky? Scared of the dark? Scared of the ghosts in that old place, eh?"

All of that in front of Chuck Wilson, and by tomorrow everybody in the whole darned town would know about it. Nick could picture that, too. The other guys teasing him the rest of the summer, maybe longer than that, about being chicken.

Better chicken than burned up in a fire some maniac arsonist set.

The thought flashed through his mind, very quickly, and was gone. He didn't *know* that there was an arsonist loose; the fire in the alley could very well have been only kids playing with matches or cigarettes. And besides, how could he ever face Mr. Haggard, or Mrs. Monihan, or even Mrs. Sylvan, if he didn't take care of their pets as he'd promised?

He didn't run this time. He walked briskly because the air was turning chilly, as it almost always did in the evening, and thought out how he would explain it all to his father tomorrow.

As he came alongside the Hillsdale Apartments, he saw Mr. Griesner standing in the yard, and that investigator from the fire department was with him. Nick's footsteps slowed.

The red gas can lay on its side, almost concealed in the shrubbery against the side of the house. Its contents had spilled out; he could smell the gas slightly even from out here on the sidewalk.

Both men stopped talking and turned to look at him. Mr. Howard cleared his throat. "Hello, Nick. Is this the can you thought you saw in the closet in the front hall?"

Even then, with his stomach suddenly cramping in apprehension, Nick resented the choice of words. *Thought he saw?* The can was in plain sight, so they must admit now that there had been a can, at least.

"Yes. It looks like the same one." Nick's voice wavered, and he quickly brought it under control. His fingerprints were on the can, his and Sam's, and for all he knew they might be the *only* fingerprints on the thing. He cleared his throat. "We found it—Sam and I, Saturday night in Mr. Haggard's apartment. Under his sink, when we went to get out the dog food. I didn't think that was a good place to keep it, so I . . . I brought it outside, and put it down there on the side-

114

walk, by the bushes. I meant to tell someone about it, but I forgot."

"*You* brought it out here?" Mr. Howard was looking at him with narrowed eyes, or so it seemed to Nick. "Did you pour gas over the shrubs, here, or on those back steps into Mr. Griesner's apartment?"

Nick's apprehension curdled into outright fear. "No, sir. All I did was put it down on the sidewalk, where I figured it couldn't hurt anything until someone could dispose of it. It wasn't spilled anywhere; the cap was on it, tight."

Mr. Griesner spoke crossly, only for once it seemed that the annoyance was directed at someone other than Nick. "I told you, I heard a ruckus about three o'clock Saturday morning. I got up and looked out my back door—that side door, I mean—and didn't see anybody, so I just made sure everything was locked the way it's supposed to be, and I went back to bed. I figured it was some punk taking a short cut who ran into something. I didn't know it was the gas can sitting there. We have trouble every once in a while with guys cutting across here. Sometimes I hear one of them trying the doors, just to see if I've been stupid enough to leave it open. Kids, looking for something to rip off. Might have found it yesterday, but I was gone to my daughter's most of the day."

"Kids," Mr. Howard said thoughtfully. "But you didn't see anybody?"

"I only heard him," Mr. Griesner repeated.

"I—we heard something about that time, too," Nick said. "It woke us up, and Rudy growled. And Maynard, upstairs, he barked, too."

He almost told them he'd been convinced the sounds were *inside* the house, not outside. Now he wasn't so certain of that, and he didn't want Mr. Howard to think he was making up things to turn suspicion away from himself.

"Yeah, I heard the mutt upstairs," Mr. Griesner confirmed. "I tell you, if this place belonged to me, I wouldn't allow any pets. Nuisance, they are. Always making noise."

"The dogs often bark at night then?" Mr. Howard asked.

"No, no, not very often. Just once in a while, when somebody cuts through the yard at night and runs into a garbage can or, like Saturday night, that gas can. I just don't like animals much. They're dirty," Mr. Griesner said, in a tone that allowed for no other opinion.

"Well, if you found the gas can in Mr. Haggard's apartment, that explains why it wasn't still in the closet," Mr. Howard said. For the first time he smiled a little.

This wasn't reassuring, however, since Nick had to reply to that with another negative. "I asked him, this afternoon at the hospital, and Mr. Haggard said he didn't put it there. He didn't know how it got there."

Mr. Howard's smile vanished. "His apartment is kept locked, isn't it? Of course, you have a key, don't you, Nick." That part wasn't a question.

"Sure, I have a key. And I do keep it locked, except that once Sam and I came back from walking Rudy and it was unlatched. I don't know what happened that time, but we didn't see any sign anybody had been in there, or taken anything."

"Was the gas can there then?"

"I don't know. I never looked. I didn't see it before

Saturday night, and then it was Sam who discovered it. He was looking for the dog food and opened the wrong door first."

Mr. Howard smiled again, but there was a frostiness about him, as if he never quite believed anything that anybody said. "I see. Well, the streetlights have been repaired after somebody shot them out, probably with a BB gun, the trash has been moved from the alley, and there's no longer a can of gasoline on the premises. It should be safe around here now, anyway, even if we don't pin down what happened the other night."

That should have been reassuring. Nick wasn't at all certain that he felt reassured, though, as he went on into the house. He took care of Eloise first, to get that over with. It took him half an hour. And he wasn't sure how much of the stuff he got into her. Then he went down to Mr. Haggard's place, and Rudy heard him coming and yelped a welcome as he manipulated the keys in the lock.

The workmen were there again, with a ladder leaning against the wall; they came from the back of the house as Nick and Rudy headed out for a walk.

"Hey, kid, the manager don't answer his door," the one called Al said. "Tell him we found the short in the wiring, but we can't fix it until tomorrow, OK? So the lights here in the hall and on the porch won't work until then. I think it probably puts the lights out in that apartment there, too. Try the switch and see, will you?"

Nick obediently paused to try Mr. Haggard's lights. Nothing.

Al nodded. "I thought so. Wiring's old in this place. Really ought to be rewired completely, but I don't reckon Mr. Hale will spring for a big job like that. We'll take care of this on Saturday, when we can be here all day." He paused to look more intently at Nick. "Nobody living in that apartment right now anyway, is there? Old man's in the hospital or something?"

"Yes," Nick agreed, and knew *he* wasn't going to stay there without lights, either.

Al kicked at the ladder leaning beside the door. "You think it's OK if I leave this here overnight? We'll have to use it tomorrow again."

"Yeah," Greg assured him. "It's off to the side, nobody's going to trip on it. We'll have to work in the attic next time we come. I hope the people right under us won't get perturbed because of the hammering and everything. Nobody home there right now, is there?"

"Mrs. Monihan's visiting in Chicago," Nick said. "I don't know about Clyde and Roy. They usually play loud music when they're home."

"OK. I guess we won't bother them too much. See you, kid."

Nick couldn't work up much enthusiasm for walking Rudy that evening, and several times the Airedale caught him off balance, pulling him to one side as Rudy investigated something interesting. Once it was a glob of some unsavory looking garbage that the dog gulped down before Nick could stop him; another time they plunged into a tangle of berry vines after a half-glimpsed cat.

"Come on, Rudy, cut it out," Nick said, but he couldn't put conviction into that, even.

All he could think about was spending the night in the Hillsdale Apartments, alone. Without Sam. Without anybody.

He didn't have to, he reminded himself. He could still go home.

Sure, he could. And have Barney and Chuck wanting to know why, and laughing at him. And then telling every kid in town that Nick was chicken, a coward.

By the time they returned to the house, Nick had made up his mind to call his father. He'd have to wait until nine-thirty, or maybe ten, before his father would be home from bowling. He'd tell him the whole thing, and then, Nick thought, already beginning to know relief, his father would take over and do what was sensible. It was too much of a decision for a kid not quite twelve years old.

The workmen had left not only the ladder but a tool box and some other junk in the entryway. Boy, if anybody tried moving through here with the lights out, they'd break their necks. Or at least a toe. Nick paused long enough to shift the tool box closer to the wall.

Rudy raced to his dishes, plunging his nose into the water, slurping noisily, then letting his beard drip on the floor afterward, as he always did. He stood looking at Nick, then.

"I'll get it," Nick said, and stopped. For there was food in the food dish, the little pellets that were supposed to look like dried meat.

Nick scowled. He didn't remember putting anything in the dish except this morning, and the dog usually ate everything immediately. After the evening walk the only thing Rudy got was his dog biscuit.

Rudy was watching him, tongue hanging out as he panted, though since they'd hardly run at all this time there was no reason for him to be tired out.

He was waiting for his "cookie." With a sigh, wondering if old-age forgetfulness was catching, Nick got out the box and fed Rudy his treat. Then Rudy bent down and finished the food in the dish. Without vitamins? Nick wondered. Then decided the pellets must be left over from breakfast.

Nick left him there and went up the stairs. It was still light outside, though growing gloomy within, and he tried out his little pocket flashlight, which he had remembered tonight, just to be sure he didn't get caught here in the pitch dark later on with dead batteries.

As he entered Mrs. Monihan's living room, Fred rose and stretched, meowing a greeting. Usually Maynard yipped a welcome, too, but this time he didn't. The fluffy little dog stood in the doorway to the kitchen, giving only a tentative wag of his tail as Nick walked toward him.

"What's the matter?" Nick said. "You think I forgot to feed you?"

The lights were all right here, he was glad to see. And then he stared down at the colored bowls along the wall. Was he losing his mind, or what? There was still food in Maynard's dish, too, though it wasn't full.

And there was . .

He almost stepped in it before he realized what was in the middle of the kitchen floor. Maynard had upchucked his dog food; it hadn't even begun to digest, yet, but that didn't make it any less repulsive.

Nick made a sound of disgust, and Maynard gave another feeble wag of his tail, waiting for Nick to scold him, perhaps.

"What's making you sick?" Nick demanded. "You were OK this morning."

The brushy tail drooped.

"Well, I guess you can't help being sick. And at least you didn't throw up on the rug." Nick looked around for something to use to clean up the mess, and told himself firmly that he would *not* be sick himself, doing it. Fred came and brushed against him as he knelt, purring his pleasure that their keeper had come. No doubt Mrs. Monihan was right after all, the animals did get lonesome when they were left alone for hours and hours.

"OK," Nick told him. "I'll stay up here with you until it's time to call my dad. We'll watch TV together or something."

Maynard had dropped onto his belly and regarded Nick through the dirty-looking strands of hair that hung over his eyes.

"You feeling better now?" Nick asked. He rubbed the small head, and Maynard licked at his hand, grateful for the attention. "I don't know if you're sick enough so we should pass up the walk, or not. I hope you're not going to be *really* sick, so you need a vet or anything."

Nick reached for the leash, just to see if Maynard acted interested in their usual evening excursion, and Maynard stood up at once. Yes, he'd have to go out in the alley for a few minutes, anyway. If he didn't seem very spritely, Nick would simply bring him back after that.

Maynard wasn't quite up to par, but he trotted along as if with purpose, not to be deprived of his exercise; they went down the alley through the block, and then around and back down Hillsdale Street. Though Maynard was reassuringly normal-acting by the time they returned, Nick decided that was enough for tonight.

Maynard barked as they went in the front door. Not

a warning bark, only a sharp little yap, acknowledging someone he recognized, maybe.

Though the streetlight had come on, as on Saturday night very little of the illumination penetrated the entryway. For once Rudy wasn't whining on the other side of the door because of Nick's arrival; there was only silence. Nick's flashlight made a narrow yellow band across the worn linoleum at the foot of the stairs.

"Nick, is that you?"

He jumped, for he hadn't heard anyone coming. The light focused on a pair of stockinged feet, then rose up the bean-pole length of Mrs. Sylvan, who was clutching Eloise against her chest.

"What on earth is going on with the lights in this place?" she demanded, as if he were personally responsible for the lack of them. "All I have is a bathroom light. Everything is off in my living room and kitchen. Poor Eloise was alone in the dark when I got home, and now I can't even put my feet up and read or watch a little television before I go to bed. I knocked on Mr. Griesner's door but he didn't answer. I suppose he's gone over to his daughter's for dinner; he sometimes does that on a Monday night."

Imagine Mr. Griesner having a daughter. Nick hadn't thought him the sort of person who had any relatives, especially younger ones. Though come to think of it, he had mentioned being at his daughter's yesterday.

"Some men have been here, making repairs," Nick explained. He felt Maynard's slight weight settle onto his right foot, warming it. "There's something wrong with the wiring, that's why the hall light kept going out, and they can't fix it until tomorrow."

He had the flash trained on her midsection, so as not to

blind her, but he could see her face above the circle of light. Her thin lips were pinched together, her expression exasperated.

"And we're supposed to get along until tomorrow without any electricity? I can't even make myself a cup of tea. Is the power off in the whole house?" And then, before Nick could reply, she asked, "Is there power in Mr. Haggard's apartment?"

"No, ma'am. It's off there, too." He could have volunteered that the stove was working in Mrs. Monihan's apartment, but he didn't really want to.

She made a furious snorting sound. "If apartments everywhere weren't so expensive, I'd be tempted to move out. There's always something malfunctioning around here. Well, I'm not going to sit in a cold, dark room, with no tea, until bedtime. And then not be able to have a hot breakfast, either."

She shifted the fluffy white cat so that its head rested against her chin, her fingers buried deep in the soft fur. "I'm going to call my sister and invite myself over there for the night. I can't take Eloise, though. They have a monstrous, ill-mannered dog who terrifies her. So would you mind giving her the last dose of medicine tonight?"

Nick stared at her, his heart sinking. After his half hour struggle earlier, he had no desire to tangle with Eloise again. "It's getting harder and harder to get it into her," he said now. "She knows what I intend to do, and she always runs away." He didn't mention that Eloise had climbed furniture and curtains to escape, and that he had the feeling it was dangerous to turn his back on her for fear she'd jump on him and bite his neck. "I was hoping she'd be better pretty soon and not need the medicine any more."

"Has she been giving you trouble? Poor baby, I'm sure it frightens her."

No more than Eloise frightened him, Nick thought; the way she looked at him he wouldn't have been surprised if she'd gone for his eyes.

"I brought home a cat carrier," Mrs. Sylvan said. "To take her to the veterinarian tomorrow. If he says she's better now, we can stop the medication. I didn't have a carrier before, and it was very traumatic for Eloise; the other animals disturbed her, and it was all I could do to hold her. So this time she'll travel in the box, which should be easier on her."

Not to mention easier on anyone who had to handle her. "Is it too early to give her the last dose now? I mean, then you could put her in the cage ahead of time, for the night," Nick suggested. "While I'm here to help, in case she doesn't want to get into it."

Mrs. Sylvan considered, stroking her pet as she did so. "It's too soon. I don't want her shut up in a box all night. I'll manage all right in the morning."

"I sure hope she's better," Nick said with feeling, "and can stop taking the medicine." And then, because the woman gave him an odd look, he wondered if he'd sounded so fervent about it that she guessed how much he'd hated administering that medication.

It was nine-thirty by the time Nick got Maynard back upstairs. He dialed his own number and to his surprise got, not Barney, but Winnie.

"What are you doing still up?" he demanded.

"I was in bed," Winnie admitted, sounding very young over the telephone. "Barney and Chuck are out in the garage, so I answered the phone when it rang. We made fudge, Nick. It got hard so fast we could hardly get it out of the pan, but it tastes good. I saved you some."

"That's more than Barney would have done. Thanks," Nick told her. "I guess Dad's not home yet, then, or Mom, either."

"No. Mom called and said she was meeting Dad after bowling, and the team was going out for pizza. She's going to bring me a piece."

Pizza. Nick groaned. The bowling team didn't usually stay out past ten, at the latest, but on the nights when they won big, or when they got beaten so badly they needed something to make them feel better, they sometimes went to the Pizza Palace. Nick knew from experience that it might make it midnight before they came home.

He hadn't realized quite how much he was counting on his father's counsel until he learned that it wasn't available.

Well, Nick thought, it wasn't as if Dad wouldn't be home later. It didn't mean he'd have to spend the night here, only a few more hours. He just wished he was more certain that nothing bad would happen during that time.

IO

N I C K swallowed. "Listen, Winnie. Tell Dad, when he comes in, that I need to talk to him." Nick realized at once that that wouldn't work, because Winnie would be asleep by then. "Get a paper and pencil, and I'll spell out a message. You can stick it up on the refrigerator so he'll see it when he comes in, OK?"

It seemed the best he could do. Nick turned from the phone to see that Maynard had already curled up on the rug before the couch where Fred slept draped over one arm.

Nick turned on the TV and sat down to watch it. There wasn't much of anything on that he hadn't already seen except a horror show about a monster that lived in a pond and came out at night to drag its victims down into the swamp.

It might have been all right to watch if Sam had been with him; tonight, Nick decided, he didn't need anything like this. He got up and turned off the set.

He stood for a moment, looking out at the lighted

windows in the house next door. He was glad that Melody's family had moved in, or he'd have been looking at dark, blank windows, making him feel even more alone than he already felt.

Suddenly, across the hall, loud music boomed. Well, that meant Clyde and Roy were home, so he wasn't alone, after all. It made him feel somewhat better.

Directly across from him, Melody appeared in one of the lighted windows. She reached up to draw the shade, saw him, and waved.

Nick waved back, wondering if she thought he was a peeping tom or something. It was embarrassing, to be caught looking into her window at night. And then Melody raised the window and leaned out, so Nick did the same. They weren't really very far apart, no more than four or five yards.

"Hi! Are you still taking care of that cat?"

"Two cats and two dogs," Nick confirmed. She didn't sound annoyed at finding him there. In fact, she was smiling as if she were pleased.

"Dad says we can get a dog, now that we're settled in one place. Dickie and I have been trying to decide what kind we want. A big one, like that Airedale, or a little one. Which is the best?"

"Depends on what you want. If you're going to walk him yourself, maybe you'd be happier with one Maynard's size. He can't drag you off into the blackberry bushes or jerk you off a curb when you aren't expecting it."

"Maynard, is that the little one's name?" Melody had a nice laugh. She leaned on her elbows on the window frame. "Funny name for a dog, isn't it? Well, we don't have a yard for a dog, so I guess we'd have to walk him all right. Do you know of any place to get a small dog?"

"There's a pet shop on the mall, but I think they have only pedigreed dogs and they're pretty expensive." Nick had an inspiration. "I know some people whose dog just had puppies. Dad said we couldn't have one, but maybe they'd give one to you. They aren't pedigreed, though. The mother is a little bigger than Maynard, sort of a cross between a poodle and cocker spaniel. The pups are real cute."

"Cockapoos," Melody said. "Will you ask if we can go look at them?"

"Sure," Nick agreed. "Maybe we could go over there tomorrow. It's only about a mile and a half, if you don't mind walking that far."

Melody grinned. "Thanks." She turned her head to call behind her, "All right, I'm coming," and then waved out the window. "Goodnight, Nick."

She didn't close the window behind her, nor did she turn off the light. There were few insects in this part of California, and most people didn't bother with screens. Nick could see into her room after Melody had left it, and though he knew she'd gone somewhere else, it was nice to see a lighted window so close by. If he hollered, anybody over there would surely hear him.

Now why had he thought a dumb thing like that? He wasn't going to holler, was he?

He ate the last of the cookies Mrs. Monihan had left, offering the final bite to Maynard, who was usually capering around his feet waiting for his share.

Tonight Maynard opened one eye and looked at the half-cookie on the rug. He licked at it listlessly but did not eat it.

"Hey, you sick or something? Really sick?" Nick

looked uneasily at the little dog. Maynard had thrown up, after all, though dogs sometimes did that without having anything seriously wrong.

"You sure you don't want any?" He held the tidbit close to Maynard's nose, which twitched. Maynard's tail thumped once, but he still didn't eat the cookie.

It was one more thing he'd mention to his father, when the time came. Maybe Dad would come over and look at Maynard. Nick touched the black button nose. It wasn't hot. He didn't know if that proved anything or not. Maynard had gone back to sleep.

Nick sighed. He supposed it was late enough so that he should go downstairs and give Eloise her last dose of medicine. He hoped it was the last one he ever had to give her, that the vet would pronounce her cured.

The music followed him down the dark stairs as he probed his way with the little flashlight. Booming, crashing, throbbing music, the kind his mother said gave her a headache. Clyde and Roy had seemed nice enough, but they certainly weren't very considerate of their neighbors.

Again Rudy didn't whine or claw at the door when Nick went past. He must finally understand that he didn't get to go out, Nick decided, every time he was nearby.

It didn't dawn on him until he had the key in Mrs. Sylvan's door that he was expected to capture Eloise in the dark. True, the bathroom light could be turned on, but Eloise had long since learned that heading for that small room gave Nick the advantage in their battle of wits and strength. Eloise might be a real pain in the neck, but she wasn't stupid.

Resentment against Mrs. Sylvan rose inside him. It

wasn't fair that she expected him to do what she wasn't willing to do herself.

He should have told her, he thought. He unlocked the door, listened to make sure Eloise wasn't just on the other side, and slowly eased the door open, with the light trained on the widening crack.

Nick was halfway into the apartment when the big puff of white fur bolted past him. There was no way he could move fast enough to block her escape.

He muttered a word that his mother had once washed out his mouth with soap for saying, when he was little, and swung the flashlight to follow Eloise's passage. Up the stairs, he saw that much. He said another bad word.

He was about to close the door to the apartment when he saw the cat box. Mrs. Sylvan thought it was too early to put Eloise into it and leave her for the night, but he'd be darned if he was going to chase her all over and get scratched to shreds. If he could corner her, Eloise was going into the cat box.

Nick grabbed it up and ran up the stairs, arriving on the second floor in time to see Eloise make a dash from a perch on the upper railing into the open doorway of the front apartment.

Roy had just opened that door, and he reeled backward with a yelp as Eloise catapulted past his left ear. Beyond him, in the lighted room, there was another yelp, followed by an oath considerably worse than the ones Nick had used.

"What was that?" Roy demanded.

"Quick, shut the door so she can't get out," Nick pleaded. "I've got to catch her in this box."

Clyde was still swearing, and when Nick entered the door he saw why.

Clyde was kneeling to paint on a huge canvas laid flat on the floor. Eloise had landed in an area freshly painted scarlet—Nick couldn't quite make out what it was supposed to be—and now there were bloody looking footprints across not only the canvas Clyde was working on but the top one of a stack of three more alongside it.

Eloise, still fleeing her pursuer, skidded to a stop in a corner and turned to arch her back and spit.

For a moment Nick was too distracted by the damage done to Clyde's painting to notice. "Oh, no! Oh, gosh, look what that stupid cat's done!"

"Do you know what I had to pay for this canvas?" Clyde demanded, sitting back on his bare heels. "Not to mention the paint. And the fact that a guy said he'd buy it if I could get another sunset like the one I sold his neighbor."

Nick couldn't think what to say to that. Was he responsible? Or was Mrs. Sylvan? If he had to pay for the canvas and paint, let alone the lost value to the painter, he'd never contribute another cent to the Disneyland fund for the rest of the summer.

"Hey," Roy said, staring down at the result of Eloise's flight, "you know, that's kind of interesting. You got another canvas, man, you can do another sunset. But stand up and look at that. Cat footprints in bright red. You suppose you could get her to walk in the blue paint and add some contrasting prints?"

Clyde stood up and surveyed the canvas. "Maybe you're right. It is . . . different, isn't it?"

Nick watched the two of them in amazement. Were they serious?

"With those to use to copy, I could do the blue ones

myself," Clyde said, almost under his breath. "Or black. I think it would be more dramatic with black."

He dropped back to his knees and began twisting the cap off a tube of acrylic paint.

Nick gave up. As long as they didn't expect him to pay for damages, he didn't care how crazy the picture turned out. He began to edge toward Eloise, who was more or less trapped in a corner of the kitchenette.

Nick wondered if he could rush her and capture her without getting scratched. There ought to be extra pay on a job that required bleeding.

"Hey, kid, you're going about that wrong," Roy informed him.

Nick noticed for the first time then that Roy hardly looked like a hippie at all tonight, except for his long hair in the ponytail, which was tied with a red bandana handkerchief. He wore new jeans and a colorful western shirt with a suede vest. And he was no longer barefooted; on his feet were a pair of the most elaborately tooled cowboy boots imaginable, with little heels and sharply pointed toes that almost made Nick wince to look at them.

"What you do, see, is entice the cat into the box, not try to pop it over her. She'll tear you to shreds if you do that. See how she's looking at you?"

"I tried enticing her when I first met her," Nick said tiredly. "She's suspicious of everything I do."

"Here," Roy offered, reaching for the cardboard cat container. "Let me try. I'll put something in there to tempt her, and we'll just let her take her time getting it. Let her wander around, if she wants to. Maybe she'll make some more of those neat footprints. Put out some more paint, Clyde, in case she walks back in your direction."

Nick had no objection to trying Roy's method, though he wasn't too hopeful that it would work. At the moment, pressed against the wall with her back arched and ready to strike at anything that came within her reach, Eloise didn't seem likely to be caught in any trap. She was a tough customer.

Even half a fish stick rescued from the garbage didn't immediately lure Eloise into the box laid on its side before her, though they saw her nose quiver as the scent of it reached her.

"Leave her alone for a while. Pretend you aren't paying any attention," Clyde suggested.

"Only stay ready to leap when she gets her head inside the box," Roy added. "Hey, man, you're making better footprints than the cat did. That's going to make a fantastic painting."

Nick turned then to watch Clyde as he painstakingly reproduced the red footprints, only in black, making approving sounds to himself. At least he wasn't going to demand to be paid for a ruined canvas, Nick thought.

Clyde nodded absently, bent over his work. "Maybe I'll enter this one in the Art Fair. What do you think?"

"Sure, why not? Last year one of the prizes went to a ceramic tongue, twice normal size; this has more class than that. Who knows, you might win a prize. Five hundred dollars, if you take first place."

Clyde, Nick now observed, had also added new garments to his wardrobe. Jeans, already with a smudge of red paint on one knee, and one of those flowered shirts like you saw in the commercials for Hawaiian holidays.

"Well, we only got about two hundred bucks left, after we bought the car and everything," Clyde said, rocking back on his heels to examine his handiwork. "Hey, look, I think she's going for it."

Sure enough, when the attention turned away from her, Eloise had deflated to her normal size and was slowly sneaking up on the fish stick as if it were a mouse. When she put her head cautiously inside the open end of the box, Roy moved, fast.

"There you are! One cat in a box," he said, laughing, and handed it over to Nick.

Eloise didn't take kindly to the container; for a minute or so she thrashed around inside and complained noisily, but the lid was latched down. Nick decided he didn't care what Mrs. Sylvan thought, he wasn't going to let Eloise out of the box before morning. There would be no medicine tonight. And if Eloise still needed medication after she saw the vet tomorrow, he was going to tell Mrs. Sylvan that he was resigning from the job.

"Thanks," he told Roy, meaning it. "I'll get her out of here, now."

"If Clyde wins a prize with this canvas, bring her back to make some more pictures," Roy suggested. He reached for the control on the stereo, and the abrupt cessation of the throbbing music left Nick feeling strangely unbalanced, as if it had actually been holding him up. "Come on, Clyde, if you're going to come and hear me play, let's go. I gotta be there in half an hour, man."

"OK, OK, just let me finish this." Clyde applied the final touch to another footprint and stood up. "See you later, kid."

They clattered down the stairs ahead of him, making the sort of racket his mother complained about when Nick and Barney did it. And then they were out the front door, and he heard their van starting up. Nick stood on the landing with the cat box in his arms, his flashlight beam very tiny in the vast darkness of the entryway.

He heard no sounds at all except his own breathing. And that seemed odd to him, because ordinarily Rudy would have given some sign that he knew Nick was there.

Slowly, hugging the cat box against his chest with one hand while he focused the light with the other, Nick went the rest of the way down the stairs. "Rudy?" he said, close to the door of Mr. Haggard's apartment.

There was no sound behind the door.

Nick put down the cat box, making Eloise mew another protest as her position shifted, but he wasn't thinking about Eloise. He unlocked the door and shone the light into the apartment.

Rudy lay on the rug before the couch, not moving. Nick suddenly felt as if his blood had thickened so that it couldn't move through his veins, except where it pounded in his ears.

"Rudy?" he said again, louder this time.

The big Airedale didn't move.

II

N I C K ran quickly across the room and dropped to his knees beside the dog. "Rudy? Are you OK?"

The dog opened one eye, to Nick's vast relief, but he didn't lift his head. Only when Nick stroked his warm flank did Rudy's tail flicker, just barely.

"There's something the matter with you," Nick said.

He'd spent plenty of time in this apartment lately, but it was different with no lights on. It no longer seemed a pleasant place.

He continued to kneel, stroking the dog, speaking to him. Rudy was breathing all right; and when Nick put his ear to the dog's side, he could hear his heart beating. Yet this was completely out of character, for Rudy to lie still this way, to respond so faintly when spoken to. Not even to bark at Eloise!

Nick rose and got down the choke chain, slipping it over Rudy's head. Always before, Rudy had gotten excited at the mere jangle of the chain, knowing he was going out. This time, he simply closed his eyes and went back to sleep.

Nick felt a moment of panic. Something had to be seriously wrong. "Come on, boy, get up!" he urged, tugging the chain. "Come on, Rudy, let's go for a walk!"

It took several minutes to get the dog on his feet. "Come on. I can't leave you down here, and Maynard's sick upstairs, so I can't leave him all alone, either . . ."

His voice sounded too loud in the empty room. Both dogs sick at the same time? Wasn't that a most peculiar coincidence?

Rudy took a few wobbly steps with him toward the hallway as Nick's mind raced. Could someone else have fed both dogs? Something that made them both sick?

Who? Did someone else have keys to both apartments? And why would anybody want to make the dogs sick?

The house was so still. Unless Mr. Griesner was home, Nick thought, he was alone here with the animals. The realization made him break out in goose bumps. He'd been home alone in the dark lots of times, and he'd never given it any thought. He certainly hadn't been scared.

He was scared now.

Nick dropped the leather handle on the chain and patted Rudy's head. "Stay, boy," he said, and went back along the hallway to Mr. Griesner's door.

There was no crack of light under it. Nick knocked, anyway, just in case. There was no reply, and after a moment he turned and went back to the front entryway.

Should he take Rudy out and try to walk him as far

as his own home? Realistically, he didn't think Rudy could walk that far, the way he was, and even if Nick got the dog there, he'd still be on his own. His parents wouldn't be home for hours, maybe.

Ordinarily, if his parents weren't available in an emergency, he'd have called his grandmother, only she was in the hospital. And even if he could get Rudy anywhere, it would mean leaving the other animals here.

That didn't seem like a very good idea, to leave them alone in the house.

In the end, he took Rudy and Eloise upstairs, one at a time, after he'd shut Fred into Mrs. Monihan's bathroom. With Eloise in her cat box, he decided it ought to work all right to have them all together. After all Maynard and Rudy got along all right, even when they weren't sick.

Rudy walked up the stairs as if he'd had too much to drink; and when Nick let go of the leash, he sank down at once, just inside Mrs. Monihan's apartment.

Maynard opened an eye and thumped his tail halfheartedly without getting up.

Something was terribly wrong with the dogs. More to try something, anything, than from a conviction that Rudy was thirsty, Nick offered him water. To his surprise, Rudy lapped at it eagerly, and then Maynard did the same, but it didn't make any difference. Each immediately went back to sleep.

In the bathroom Fred scratched and protested being put into solitary confinement; Eloise replied with scratching of her own, and Nick hoped her claws wouldn't tear the box apart from the inside.

He tried once more to call his father, just in case he'd come home earlier than expected and hadn't seen the note Winnie had left for him. There was no answer at all, though Nick let it ring and ring.

Which meant, he hoped, that Winnie had gone to sleep and Barney and his friend were in the garage where they didn't hear the telephone. He hoped they hadn't gone off and left Winnie alone, when they were supposed to be watching out for her.

Melody's window across the way was dark now. Had she gone to bed? The window was still open, anyway.

Nick wanted to yell at her, call her to the window, just to make contact with *somebody*. What could he say, though, that wouldn't sound idiotic? And she'd think he was a sissy, afraid to be alone in a house.

He turned away from the window and switched on the TV again. He had to have some sound in the place besides the quiet breathing of the two dogs.

For a few seconds he didn't know why the face that appeared on the television screen was familiar, and then he recognized the man. Mr. Hale, who owned the Hillsdale Apartments. He was making a speech about something to do with protection of the county's natural resources.

Nick wanted the trees and the beaches preserved, but he didn't care to listen to a speech on the subject. He changed the channel and was back in the middle of the horror movie. The monster was sucking down into the swamp a girl with torn clothes who was shrieking and kicking.

Nick muttered under his breath and turned the dial again, then pushed the button to turn the set off. What was he going to do to keep from going crazy until his dad got home?

He jumped when Rudy began to make peculiar

sounds. Gagging, Nick realized, and he tried to get the dog on his feet, to head him toward the kitchen, off the living room carpet.

He didn't quite make it. Nick felt a prickling in his eyes, as if he were going to cry, though of course that was absurd. An almost-twelve-year-old didn't cry just because a dog threw up on a carpet, even if he did have to clean it up.

He gritted his teeth and did the job, thinking of Barney mowing lawns out in the fresh air and getting better money for it.

Rudy went to Maynard's water dish and lapped at it, then stood, his expression groggy, staring at Nick as if in apology.

Nick melted. He put an arm around Rudy's neck, sitting there on the floor beside him, and hugged him. "Poor old guy. What's happened to you, anyway? You and Maynard both. What did you get hold of? I know you ate one glob of garbage out there in the alley, but that was a long time ago. I hope you're not both getting some disease or something. When my dad calls, I'll have him take a look at you both, and maybe we'll call a vet."

Rudy licked at his ear and wagged his stumpy tail. When Nick stopped patting him, he staggered onto the carpet again and went back to sleep.

Nick tried once more to call home, once more got no answer, and in disgust stretched out on the couch to wait for his father to come home. He had to move Maynard aside to have room for his feet; when he was settled in, Maynard snuggled against his ankles, a welcome warmth there.

He wasn't sure if he'd dozed off or not. But all of a sudden he sat straight up, listening.

There were footsteps coming up the stairs, slowly, carefully.

The only light he had on was a little lamp over the TV, which didn't give a great deal of illumination. It was enough, however, for him to see the clock beside it. A quarter of eleven. Early for Roy and Clyde to be coming home if Roy was playing guitar for the evening at one of the night spots where he worked.

It didn't sound like Roy and Clyde, at least not the way they usually took the stairs. Of course the lights were out, and they hadn't had a flashlight, he remembered. He'd lighted their way downstairs with his own.

Who else could it be, though? Nobody else ever came up here, not even Mr. Griesner except to bang on the door and yell about turning down the music.

Rudy and Maynard just went on sleeping. No barking tonight because someone was in the hall. Did that mean they recognized who it was and accepted them? Or were they in such a heavy sleep that they weren't even aware of the sounds?

Nick dropped a hand onto Rudy's head, but the Airedale slumbered on. Nick's mouth was suddenly dry, because the dog was sleeping too soundly for it to be normal. Ordinarily he would have responded to such a touch.

Drugged, he thought. Were they drugged? Had there been something in that garbage Rudy ate in the alley? Or in the dog food both dogs had had in their dishes?

He really didn't remember putting anything out for them since breakfast, and yet there had been food left, though neither of them had ever failed to clean up his bowl almost at once.

Why was his mind working so clearly now, when he

hadn't thought of it earlier? Had the dog food had something in it to make the dogs sleep, or to make them sick? He thought if it had been a poison that would kill them, it would have done so before this. Poisons usually worked fast, didn't they? He wondered if throwing up part of what they'd eaten meant they'd gotten rid of part of it; he sure hoped so.

They'd had enough to make them sleep through just about anything, though. Nick sat on the edge of the couch, his heart beating so loudly that for a moment he couldn't tell if there was still anyone moving around out in the hall or not.

Nick eased onto his stockinged feet and moved silently toward the door, leaning his ear against it to listen.

Quite clearly he heard a key turn in the lock across the hall.

If it was Clyde and Roy returning, Nick thought, they'd turn on the stereo as soon as they turned on the lights. They always did, even at night, and they knew there was nobody home below them tonight.

There was no music.

Something clattered and fell, and a man's voice cursed.

"Gives me the creeps," another voice said.

"Crummy old place like this, it's better off being burned down."

"Come on, let's get the job done and get out of here. Wish we'd been able to do it last night. Those darn dogs! But the stuff we got today worked all right. No barking tonight to get people all riled up and investigating. Here, you take this one, and I'll take the other one."

Nick, behind the door to Mrs. Monihan's apartment,

sorted out what he was hearing. He was so cold he could hardly move. Did it mean what he thought it did?

It hurt his chest to breathe. He moved almost blindly to the telephone and dialed his own house. Still no answer. *When I get hold of Barney, I'll pound his brains out,* Nick thought. He was supposed to be baby-sitting Winnie and to stay within reach of the phone, and he knew nobody could hear it ring from the garage.

The police. He'd better call the police.

He didn't know what he'd say, didn't know if he could make them believe him, that something was terribly wrong at the Hillsdale Apartments. Maybe he should just call the fire department, if what he suspected was the truth. Whoever was out there had been here before, had been scared off by the dogs; now they'd returned to finish their job.

Had the speaker meant it literally, that the house would be better off burned down? Was that what they were here to do?

You dialed 911 for emergency calls, he knew that. He was so nervous he could hardly get his finger in the right place, and then it was too late, anyway.

Because this time the key was clicking in the lock right across the room from him, and before he could do anything else at all, the door began to swing inward.

12

AFTERWARD, he thought maybe if he'd kept his head and finished dialing the three digit number he might have summoned help even if he didn't have time to speak to the emergency operator, though the intruders would have walked in on him in the middle of the procedure.

As it was, Nick panicked.

He dropped the phone and threw himself into the only hiding place he could reach fast enough. Behind the couch.

It wasn't really much of a hiding place, because the couch stood several feet out from the wall to allow for access to a bookcase on that wall. If anybody walked to the end of the couch, there wouldn't be any hiding place at all; Nick would be in plain sight.

It was the only thing he could think of, however. He held his breath as long as he could; he couldn't do anything about his heart. It was making so much noise he was sure anyone in the room could hear it.

They didn't seem to, though. And it took only a few seconds for Nick to realize who they were.

The workmen, Al and Greg. They'd had keys; his mind registered that. They'd had keys to the front door, to Clyde and Roy's apartment, and to this one. No doubt they had keys to the others, as well, which explained how they'd gotten in and put drugged dog food into Rudy and Maynard's dishes.

As if reading his mind, Greg said, "The stuff worked. The dogs are out cold."

"Yeah. We won't have any trouble from them. Hey, did you leave a light on in here? And why are they both in the same apartment?"

"Maybe the kid was here after and put the dogs together for company. He may have left the light on, too." He sniggered. "Or maybe that cat turned it on, the way he did the stove, huh?" He laughed again. "That was a good idea I had, pulling the fuses on most of the lights so everybody'd get out of the house tonight. Worked better than just unscrewing bulbs all over the place."

Al walked toward the couch. Nick could see his feet in the narrow space between the bottom of the couch and the floor; his chest was bursting and he had to have air, so he tried to inhale very slowly and quietly. There was dust in the carpet behind the furniture and he hoped desperately that it wouldn't make him sneeze.

"Hey. The phone's off the hook."

Nick swiveled his head slightly and saw it, dangling at the end of its cord, swaying gently. Then it disappeared as Al picked it up.

"Nobody on it, just a dial tone. It was moving, though. Like somebody just dropped it."

"You probably made a breeze when you walked over there. Come on, let's pour this stuff around and get out of here. This time we're going to do it right, no slip-ups, no stupid kids finding the fire too soon, no nasty Mr. Hale wanting to know why we can't do anything right."

"If he's so particular, he should start his own fire. Burn down his own building," Al said. Nick couldn't see anybody now, but heard footsteps going toward the kitchen, and then a sloshing sound, like running water.

"Take it easy with that stuff," Al warned. "If we use too much they're going to know it was arson. Mr. nasty Hale wouldn't like that, if his alibi was all for nothing and they figure out he set this up. The insurance won't pay off if he torches his own place. It's supposed to look like an accident."

In the kitchen, Greg swore. "We've been trying to make an 'accident' for over two weeks. This time I'm just going to get it burned down, collect my money, and get out of town. If Hale gets caught, that's his problem. I'm gonna be long gone by that time."

His voice sounded closer as he returned to the living room. "If it hadn't been for that stupid kid that walks the dogs, we'd have been finished before this. We couldn't start a fire under the stairs, or under the old man's sink, or up here. He must've found the cereal box before it burned up enough to catch the curtains behind it. I figured with the lights out in the old man's apartment, though, he wouldn't stay down there again."

Nick's chest hurt so bad he didn't know how much longer he could stay frozen in this position, nor how long he could avoid sneezing, either. If his father came home and tried to call and got no answer, would he come looking for Nick, or just assume that Nick was out walking the dogs one last time?

Immediately he knew that wouldn't matter. Even if his dad called right now, he'd never get here in time. These guys were planning to start their fire any minute.

Would he have time to get out, to get the animals out, once they'd left? They surely were planning to set a fire in such a way as to allow themselves time to escape. Maybe, Nick thought, his mind racing, he could get the dogs and cats out the back door, from Mrs. Monihan's kitchen, and down that outside stairs. If the fire wasn't already coming up underneath it. And if Rudy could wake up enough to walk down such a precarious escape ladder.

"All set?" Greg wanted to know. "OK. Get ready to run, once we torch it off across the hall. Some ways, I'd rather have started it on the ground floor, because fire goes *up* so fast. But this is probably a better way. Those guys were burned out of a place once before, and when it happens again, everybody will think either they're careless with turpentine and that other junk they paint with, or they set it on purpose to collect some more insurance money."

"Yeah," Al agreed. One of them opened the door into the hallway. "We waited late enough so most of the people in the neighborhood have gone to bed. By the time anybody notices there's a fire up here, the whole place will be burning. Mr. Hale will have his total destruction so he can collect the insurance money."

"Who cares, as long as he pays us? Come on, let's go."

For a moment, just a moment, Nick thought they were going to walk out of the apartment, and he was already drawing himself up onto his hands and knees,

147

preparing to run for the back door as soon as they'd gone.

And then Al spoke again, in a soft, funny tone that lifted the hair off the back of Nick's neck.

"Hey. Hey, I think we got a problem, Greg."

"What now? What's the matter?"

"That kid that walks the dogs, remember?"

"Sure. I thought we asked if he was going to stay here tonight, and he said no."

Greg's voice was very low, and very frightening. "Then what are his shoes doing here at the end of the couch?"

Nick thought he was going to be sick, just like Maynard and Rudy.

The silence was more terrifying than anything they could have said. And then there were quick, heavy footsteps. A big hand grabbed Nick by the shirt collar and he was dragged out into the room. Kicking and hitting out with his fists didn't do any good; Al was much larger and stronger than he was, and when the man slapped him and threw him into a chair, Nick cowered there with a hand to where Al had struck him.

One of them, he never remembered which, let loose a long string of profanity.

"Now what do we do?" Al asked, sounding almost as hollow as Nick felt.

"What do you think we do? We torch the place, just like we agreed." Greg's voice was hard.

"But the kid knows who we are. He heard a lot of what we said."

"There's some rope in that tool box. Tie him to the couch, and when they find his remains, they'll figure he was asleep when it happened."

Nick's nose was bleeding. He felt the warm trickle down to his upper lip and put up a hand to smear it to one side. It was worse than the horror movie, it was like he was in some kind of nightmare; he could taste the blood, and he wondered if his nose was broken.

"Now wait a minute," Al protested, though he didn't sound strong enough to give Nick much hope. "I agreed to torch this place, but we said we'd get the people out of it, first. We waited till we knew they were all out, remember? I don't mind a little arson, but I'm not going to kill anybody. I'm not going to be wanted for murder."

Murder. Nick swiped again at the blood and wiped it on his jeans. They couldn't mean it, nobody could deliberately set a fire with a kid in the house so he'd get burned up. Could they?

They'd started the first fire in the alley, when the whole place was full of people. Maybe they hoped everybody would get out, because it was early and everybody was awake, but they couldn't have been sure of that. Nick swallowed painfully and stared at the one called Greg.

Greg was very skinny, but he wasn't wearing coveralls now and Nick could see that he had muscles. His dark hair hung in an uncombed lock over his forehead, and his mouth had a flat hardness that made Nick swallow again, even if it did hurt to do it.

Al was the one with the sandy mustache, which he was now tugging. "I mean it, Greg. I'm going to get out of here; let old Hale worry about burning down his own building. It's not me who has bad money problems, he has. At least, mine aren't bad enough so I'm going to burn down a house with a kid in it."

Nick waited, hoping against hope that Greg would decide the same way. Only Greg didn't.

"You're a fool. If we walk out now, the kid's going to tell what he knows, which is too much. Look, can't you see we don't have any choice? We already tried to torch the place before, and they can throw us in jail for *that*, even if we don't do anything else. We're leaving town anyway, aren't we? As soon as we light the match, we head out. Nobody will be looking for us, as long as this kid isn't around to shoot off his mouth. We have to do it that way, Al. Now come on, tie the kid up."

Al licked his lips. "The rope's still downstairs."

"Well, find something here if you don't want to go after it. The old lady that lives here must have belts or something. Look in the bedroom closet and see."

Beside his chair the curtains fluttered in the breeze that sent a chill into the room. Nick slid his gaze sideways, trying to tell if there was any light in the house next door, the room where Melody might be asleep. If she wasn't asleep, could she hear a conversation from over here?

She would hear if he stuck his head out the window and yelled, probably. Only they weren't going to let him do that. Still, he said loudly, "You won't get away with burning this house down. No matter where you go, they'll find you and bring you back, especially if anybody gets hurt when it happens."

"Shut up," Greg said. He stepped backward without looking, and ran into the cat box. Eloise aroused and let out a screech that was as much fury as anything else, and Greg looked startled. "What the heck's that?"

Nick didn't answer. Beside him, Rudy opened a bleary eye and Maynard raised his head.

Nick knew it was a slim chance that there was any-thing he could do against two men. He'd always hated being little and skinny, and now he wondered if it was going to kill him. No, he thought, even Barney wouldn't be able to fight off two men. Maybe there was something else he could do, though.

He couldn't fight them. But maybe—just maybe—he could outwit them. They couldn't be really smart or they wouldn't be doing something like this in the first place.

Al came back from the bedroom, empty-handed. "I couldn't find any belts. I'll have to go downstairs."

"Just make sure you come back," Greg said. "You've been in on everything I have so far, and that makes you just as guilty as I am. Even if you run now."

"I never said I was going to run," Al retorted, sound-ing sullen. Nick wished they'd get really mad at each other and take their attention completely away from him. If he had time to get to the back door, to get it un-locked before they caught him, he might make it. He didn't think they'd go ahead with their plans to set the house afire if he was running down the alley yelling his head off. They'd be too anxious to get themselves away from the scene before the police or the fire department arrived, or at least he hoped they would. He hated the idea of running off and leaving the animals, yet there was no way to save them unless he first saved himself.

"We should have pulled all the fuses, so the whole house was dark," Al said. "Then everybody would have gone somewhere else tonight. There wouldn't have been any people in the house."

"If we'd pulled all the fuses, those guys that live across the hall would have gone and looked for themselves, and they'd have screwed the fuses back in or got new ones," Greg pointed out. "Or that maintenance man would have stayed home and worked on things. He's pretty dumb, but he could figure out the fuses had been tampered with. How did we know this stupid kid would decide to spend the night?"

Nick was getting tired of being referred to as a stupid kid. He glanced at the curtains again, just as they blew inward in a billowing puff, giving him a glimpse of the darkened house next door.

It was dark, but they were over there, Melody's family. If they knew what was going on, they'd call for help. Only how could he make anyone aware of the situation he was in?

At his feet, Rudy stirred.

Hope leaped in Nick's chest. He slid to the edge of the chair and dropped a hand onto the wiry-haired head, pushing his foot against Rudy's shoulder to try to rouse him further.

The big dog lurched from his side onto his stomach, though he didn't get to his feet. Even that much movement was cause enough for alarm; when Rudy *whuffed* almost experimentally, both the would-be arsonists paused and looked at him.

"I thought you said that you gave them enough stuff in their food to knock them cold all night," Greg said uneasily. "They're waking up."

"He's a big dog. Maybe I didn't calculate the dose right." Al sounded equally uneasy. "He's not getting hostile, though. He's still dopey."

Nick didn't take time to consider whether it was safer to have them afraid of the dogs or not afraid of them. He said, "They both threw up a lot of what they ate."

His hand was still on Rudy's thick, strong neck, and he could feel the muscles growing from relaxed to rigid. His own excitement now balanced the fear that had been making his knees weak.

"Listen, we still have to—"

Nick's attention wavered. They were discussing something, not looking at him now, or Rudy. Again the curtains beside him billowed out in the breeze, and he knew he had to try something. Anything was better than being roasted like a marshmallow at a picnic the way he would be if Al and Greg went through with their plans.

Nick's fingers closed around the small antique clock from atop the television set. He was sure it was an heirloom or something valuable, but better a clock than his life and the lives of all the pets.

The next time the breeze lifted the curtains, giving him a clear shot, he threw the clock.

The crash was not very loud, but the men turned to look at him.

"What was that?" Al demanded.

Nick felt the pulses pounding in his ears. He wasn't nearly as good at pitching as Barney, though he did sometimes beat his brother playing darts. He'd tried to lob the clock through Melody's open window, and he thought it would have made more noise if he'd hit the side of the house with it. He sure hoped she was in the room, not downstairs somewhere.

"Did you do something?" Greg demanded. He looked very tall, standing above Nick on the edge of the chair.

Nick shook his head, not trusting his voice for a second, and then, when he thought Greg was going to drag him to his feet, he swallowed and tried to speak. "I think . . . I think something fell, or . . . or broke, next door."

"And we can hear it all the way over here?" Greg strode past him and pushed the curtains aside to slam down the open window. When he came back, he stepped on Rudy's foot and the Airedale lumbered to his feet with a protesting yelp.

For a moment they all stared at the dog; it was obvious that he was still under the effects of the sedation that Al had put in his food, but he was beginning to come out of it. Nick didn't feel so bad any more about having to clean up two messes. His hopes rose when Maynard yipped, too, although neither dog was behaving in a hostile manner. They had, after all, seen Greg and Al before.

In the cat box, Eloise let out a snarl that made Al draw away from the container. Nick rose slowly to his feet, feeling almost sick enough to lose his own supper, yet his head was working.

"I have to go to the bathroom," he said, and took a few steps in that direction.

"Sit down," Greg snapped, but Al shook his head.

"What difference does it make if the kid goes to the bathroom? There's only one little window, and if he goes out that he'll fall thirty feet. Let him go."

Greg gave in, shrugging. "Hurry up, then, get something to tie him up with. We better get out of here, and fast."

Nick was three steps from the chair when the telephone rang.

For a moment it was like that game they'd played when he was about six years old. Where everybody had to freeze into whatever position they were in when someone yelled "Statues."

Only this wasn't a game.

It was his father, it had to be his father. Nick made a lunge for the phone, knocking the receiver off the hook, but Greg was faster, jerking it away from him, slamming it back on the cradle before Nick could even gather enough air to cry out.

Al started toward the door. "Now we blew it for sure! Whoever that was, he could tell the phone was knocked over and then picked up. He's going to investigate, if it was somebody checking on the kid! Let's get out of here!"

Greg was distracted from Nick by the need to stop his companion from doing anything foolish. He reached out and grabbed Al by the shirt front, holding him while Nick managed a few more steps toward the bathroom.

"Don't be an idiot! We run now and we won't get ten miles before they pick us up, after the kid gives them a description. We've got five minutes, anyway, before anybody can get here, and everything's all set. That's all we need. Tie up the kid, and let's go."

Nick had made it to the bathroom door. He slammed it behind him. There wasn't any lock, which probably didn't matter much anyway. If the house was burning around him, what difference would it make if he were tied up or locked in the bathroom?

He really did have to go, but he didn't think he could. Fred rubbed against his leg, which was shaking so much Nick couldn't tell if the cat purred or not.

"When I let you out," Nick told him softly, "you're on your own, Fred."

In the living room, Maynard barked again.

The door was jerked open. "Come on," Al said. "Hurry up."

Nick drew in a deep breath, stepped through the doorway, and did the only thing he could think of.

13

F R E D had been confined long enough so that once the way was open, he shot past Nick and the startled arsonists. As he followed, Nick swooped on the cat box, flipping open the top before either of the men could stop him.

From then on, Mrs. Monihan's living room practically exploded.

Eloise erupted out of the box like that Mount St. Helens in Washington State; she was a boiling fury of white fur. Then, when she saw the room full of strangers and not one, but two, dogs and an unfamiliar cat, she went really wild.

Rudy and Maynard were still sluggish, but their instincts surfaced at once. Here was fair game, a cat, and they both rushed for the unfortunate creature. The deep bark and the shrill one intermingled in such a racket that though Greg yelled something, nobody understood what it was.

Fred, also startled by the presence of the big Airedale, retreated to the top of a bookcase with such haste that he knocked over a vase that fell with a resounding crash.

Eloise, terrified beyond measure by the apparent attack of all these monsters, undoubtedly feared for her life; she made a leap for the highest point within her reach (Fred was already on the bookcase, and perhaps he represented as big a threat to her as the dogs) which happened to be Al.

He had turned, half-crouching, when the vase broke behind him, so that he had his back to Eloise when she jumped. She landed on his shoulders and the back of his neck, digging in her claws to hold on, while the man yelled and tried to throw her off.

Nick didn't wait to see any more. For a few seconds he had a clear path to the back door, and he took it. He heard Greg shouting behind him; his fingers were already twisting at the safety lock, then tugging at the bolt, and a moment later he jerked the door open just as Greg made a lunge for him.

Afterward they could only speculate that Greg had intended to throw himself against the door, to keep Nick from escaping. If he hadn't tripped over Maynard at the last moment, he might have been able to stop when Nick threw open the door.

As it was, however, Greg went right past Nick out through the opening. Nick heard him falling, first down the steps, then rolling over the edge of the roof, and finally there was a clatter of garbage cans in the alley. When that din died away, Nick distinctly heard a moan from the darkness below.

He didn't have either the time or the desire to investigate. Behind him, dogs and cats yapped and screeched and something else went over with a horrendous noise.

Al had apparently figured out that he was not being attacked by a mob of policemen, only by the pets Nick had been tending; he bounded toward the kitchen, and for a minute Nick thought the man was still going to try to carry out the original plan, to tie Nick up and light the inflammable materials already in place, but he didn't.

He didn't even look at Nick. He went down the back stairs, making it all the way to the ground without falling, and Nick heard him cry out. "Greg? You there?"

"I think my ankle's broken! Move the truck over here and help me in it," Greg groaned.

In the distance, Nick heard sirens. The police or the fire department? He didn't care which, but he sure hoped they were coming here.

His eyes now getting used to the darkness, Nick made out the shape of the old pickup, parked behind the house for a quick getaway. Al didn't start it, however; there was a blur of his white T-shirt as he headed, instead, down the alley.

Though Greg called after him, Al had disappeared; Nick could still hear his feet, pounding on the gravel.

Lights had come on in the house next door, and others in the houses across the alley. There were also footsteps, heavy, rapid ones, on the stairs within the house.

Not more accomplices, Nick hoped, and braced himself to run down the back stairs, also, even at the risk of encountering Greg with a broken ankle.

He didn't need to do that, though. It was his father and Barney, and a moment later a fire truck with flashing red lights, followed by the police car, arrived on the scene below.

For a moment Nick watched as Greg, hopping on one foot toward the old pickup, made a try to escape. A sharp voice called out, "Stop right where you are!" and Greg, outlined in a spotlight from the police car, slowly turned to face the pair of police officers.

"Nick, are you OK?" Mr. Reed demanded. He gazed around in bewilderment. Feathers from pillows still floated in the air; curtains had been torn to shreds when Eloise climbed them to the safety of a curtain rod overhead; and Rudy was barking as he tried to get Fred to come out from under a chair. Maynard barked, as far as Nick could tell, just to keep Rudy company. "Good grief, what's been going on?"

Nick tried to tell them. He'd only gotten part of the story out when a police officer and two firemen appeared, and he had to start over from the beginning. And then he had to tell it all for a third time when Melody and her parents showed up.

"I thought they were going to burn the house down with all of us in it, so I did everything I could think of to stop them," Nick concluded, looking around at the circle of interested faces.

Melody was wearing pajamas and a bathrobe and slippers. She twisted the belt of the robe tighter and said, "I couldn't figure out what was going on over here. I heard loud voices, and I hadn't thought there was anybody here but you, so I figured it must be the television. Until that clock came sailing through my window and smashed on the foot of my bed. I looked out, then and saw a man close the window, so I ran and told my dad."

Mr. Jamison nodded. "It looked pretty fishy to me, especially when I saw that old truck parked in the alley, so I called the fire department after I got out there and smelled gasoline. It was just too suspicious after that fire in the alley only a few days ago. I called the police, too, just to be on the safe side. I was getting dressed to come over here when I heard what sounded like a three ring circus."

"And I called after I saw Nick's note," Mr. Reed said, "and it sounded as if somebody was fighting over the phone. So I called the police, too, and jumped in the car to come over here."

"One of them got away," Nick said, his head turning toward the police officer. "He may have gone over the fence down at the end of the alley, the way he did the other time. Through somebody's yard and into Spring Street."

"He didn't make it this time," the officer said. "He jumped onto a garbage can, only in the dark he didn't see that it didn't have the cover on it. He was still there when my partner arrived."

Mr. Reed looked around the room. "Well, I guess we'd better get this place straightened out. There's a lamp smashed, and the curtains are ruined—Nick, is there anything you can do to make those dogs stop barking like that?"

Nick knelt beside Rudy and tugged him away from the chair where he'd been putting his nose into the opening to smell Fred. "Come on, boy. Sit," he said, and to his surprise, Rudy did. Rudy's eyes still looked dopey; maybe that was why he obeyed.

When Rudy shut up, so did Maynard. The little mop dog seemed delighted with all the company and the at-

161

tention, wagging his whole rear end with the pleasure of it.

Mr. Jamison cleared his throat. "I guess we're all grateful that it turned out as well as it did, aren't we? Congratulations, young man, you used your head. It's late now. I think we'd better go on home, Melody, and try to get some sleep."

"OK." Melody suddenly smiled at Nick. "Are we still going to go look at those puppies tomorrow?"

"Sure," Nick agreed. "Why not?"

Barney stared after the Jamisons as they left. Mr. Reed and the policeman were trying to coax Eloise down so they could put her back in her cat box. Fred had crept to the front of the chair and stared out from under it, watching Rudy very carefully. He did not look especially frightened, only cautious.

"Hey," Barney said in a low voice. "That's a real cute girl, Nick. Who is she?"

Nick drew in a deep breath, glad nobody could tell how shaky it was. He tried to make his tone light and offhand. "Oh, she's just a girl I know," he said.

"Maybe she'd like to pay doubles with us—you, too, of course," Barney said quickly. "With me and this girl I met."

"I don't know if she plays tennis. Besides," Nick added, "we have other plans for tomorrow, anyway."

A fireman stuck his head around the edge of the hall door. "They sure were planning a conflagration, all right. They've got all kinds of stuff stacked up, ready to torch. It'll take us a while to get rid of all of it, make this place safe to be in." He addressed Nick. "What kind of artist lives over there, anyway? There's this big canvas covered with what look like cat footprints, in red and black paint."

"Yeah," Nick said. "I'm sure glad it didn't get burned up."

The fireman shook his head. "No question about this one being arson. Third one this week. With this recession, people can't sell buildings they want to get rid of, so they burn them down to collect the insurance. Would you believe that back east there was a case a few months ago where the *bank* officials hired someone to burn a building? The man buying it couldn't make the payments, so the bank had to take it back, and they didn't have another buyer. They didn't get away with it, of course. It'd be a good idea if you all got out of here now, just in case. There's still a lot of stuff to be cleaned up, and until that's done, the place is dangerous."

They looked at each other when the fireman had gone. Barney cleared his throat.

"I'll tell Chuck he'd probably better go home to sleep, I guess. You can tell me all the details, everything that happened."

Nick stared at him, amazed. Barney was speaking to him as if he were a fellow human being, and an interesting one at that.

"I wouldn't be surprised if you get your picture in the paper," Barney said, grinning. "Young Hero Saves House and Pets, or something like that. You might even get a reward."

"Not from the owner. Mr. Hale is the one who paid those guys to burn the place down. Hey! Maynard, you little crumb . . . !"

Nick pounced on his shoe, but it was too late.

Maynard had chewed the entire toe out of it, and one of the strings dangled from his mouth.

"Dad." Nick lifted the remains of the shoe. "I'm going to have to go home in my sock feet."

He didn't really feel bad about it, though. There were lots of things worse than not having any shoes.

A triumphant cry signaled Eloise's capture. Mr. Reed handed over the cat box, which was beginning to look a bit the worse for wear. "We'll have to take all the animals home with us, Nick. The firemen want to clear the building until they're certain it's safe. I guess the dogs are all right now that they've calmed down. What about that other cat?"

"I'll get him," Barney offered. He dropped to his knees and put out a hand under the chair, where Fred had continued to monitor the scene from the safety of his hiding place. "OW!" Barney jerked back his hand, nursing a long set of scratches. He glanced uncertainly at Nick. "Maybe you'd better get this one, and give me the one in the box. This must've been a tougher job than I thought."

"I think Fred will come to me," Nick said, feeling better by the minute. He paused to stick a finger through one of the air holes to stroke the soft white fur before he handed over the cat box.

"Good old Eloise," he said, and there was almost a note of affection in his voice. "Good old Eloise."

14

BARNEY was right about the newspaper story. It ran on the front page, with a picture of Nick and Sam and all the pets. Nick wasn't sure what the pet owners would think, but none of them blamed him for any of it.

Mr. Hale, the police had learned, was deeply in debt. He owned a good deal of property, but since he'd been unable to sell any of it to satisfy the debts, he decided to hire someone to burn the Hillsdale Apartments for the insurance money. If he'd picked someone brighter and more efficient than Greg and Al, or if Nick hadn't interfered, the job might well have been done successfully.

Nobody gave Nick a reward; but as a result of the newspaper story, he was offered several more jobs. In fact, he had so many that he talked Barney into accepting a couple of them. And by the middle of August, when the house was painted and the roof was nearly finished, Charles dumped the money they'd been saving onto the dining room table, and they all sat around and counted it.

"Is it enough, Daddy?" Winnie asked anxiously. "Can we afford to go to Disneyland?"

Nick held his breath when his father totaled up the figures, and then began to grin.

"Yes," he said, "I think we can."

And then, before everybody had stopped cheering, he added. "You know, this worked so well, maybe we should start planning ahead for *next* summer. Maybe if everybody kept on working and contributing to a new fund, by this time next year we could go to some place like Yellowstone."

Yellowstone National Park! Nick had seen pictures of it; it looked great.

"Let's do it," Molly said enthusiastically. "Is everybody agreed?"

They took a vote, and everybody voted yes. And then Nick had a terrible thought.

"What if," he asked, "I get stuck with giving medicine to another cat like Eloise?"

"Barney will help you, won't you Barney?" Charles asked.

Nick looked at his brother. Barney had been a little nicer to him for a few days; probably he liked being the brother of a local hero. It hadn't lasted long, of course. Just this morning they'd gotten in a wrestling match over whose turn it was to clean up the bathroom.

Still, they'd measured him a few days ago, on his birthday, the way they always did. And he'd grown an inch and a half since school was out. Barney had hardly grown half an inch, so Nick was gaining on him. One of these days, Nick thought, he was going to be as big as Barney.

"Sure," Nick said. "Barney will help me, or I'll punch him out."

"You and who else?" Barney demanded. But he didn't hit Nick right then, the way he would have early in the summer.

"Come on," Mrs. Reed said. "If we're going to Disneyland next week, we've got a lot to do. Let's get started."

All in all, Nick decided, it had been a pretty good summer.

He couldn't wait for the next one.